Tír na nÓg
A New Adventure

William Henry

Tír na nÓg
A New Adventure

Illustrations
by
Delphine Arnault

MERCIER PRESS
WHAT YOU NEED TO READ

MERCIER PRESS,
Cork
www.mercierpress.ie

Trade enquiries to:
Columba Mercier Distribution,
55a Spruce Avenue, Stillorgan Industrial Park,
Blackrock, County Dublin

ISBN: 978 1 85635 597 1

10 9 8 7 6 5 4 3 2 1

THIS BOOK WAS INSPIRED
BY NAOMI JANE ZETTL –
A WONDERFUL SPIRITUAL LADY

Mercier Press receives financial assistance from
the Arts Council/An Chomhairle Ealaíon

Printed and bound in the EU

For my darling daughter

Lisa

Touched by magic

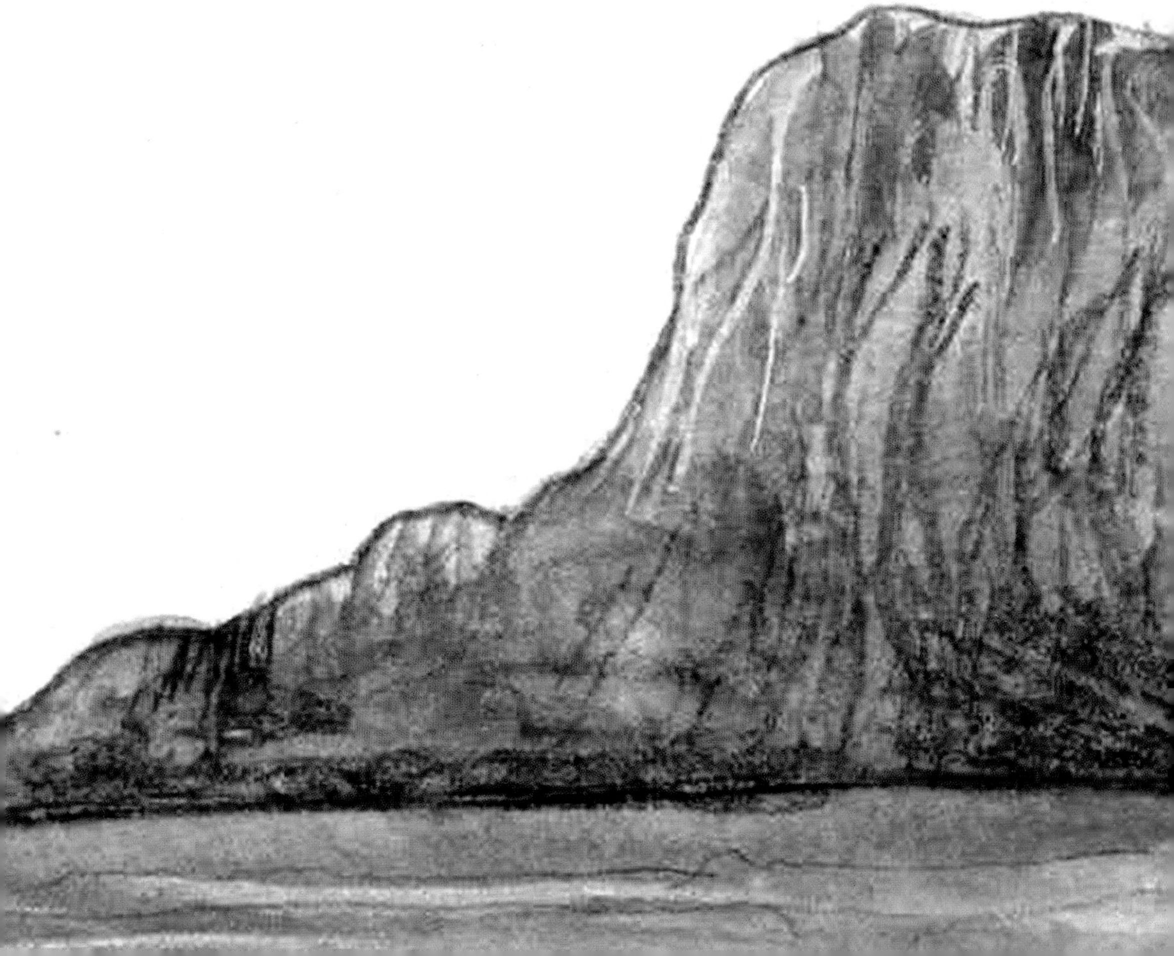

Contents

A Fabled Island

S omewhere far out upon the Atlantic Ocean off the western coast of Ireland lies a fabled island, which men have tried to reach for centuries, but have always failed. Some call it Atlantis, others call it Hy-Brasil, after an ancient Celtic chieftain whose daughter Gaillimh was drowned in the river at Galway many hundreds of years ago.

There is an old story of Spanish sailors who went in search of this island and followed it across the ocean. According to the legend, the island always remained just out of their reach and, try as they might, they could not land on its enchanted shore. After they had travelled a great distance in pursuit of this magical place, it faded before them. They did not fully realise just how far they had journeyed, but before turning their ship for home they saw a huge landmass. And so, the story goes, they landed and named this place Brasil, after the island which had led them there. Today it is known as Brazil.

Others call this mythical island Tír na nÓg, the Land of Eternal Youth, where time stands still. This is a magical island of dreams, the dream of eternal youth and happiness, sought by people since the beginning of time. Others say that this is where the Tuatha Dé Danaan sought refuge after they left Ireland and became the fairy people. It is a land now lost in the mists of Celtic legend and folklore, clouded over by the sands of time.

The sea surrounding Tír na nÓg is inhabited by mermaids, whose song is said to captivate all who hear it. Tradition tells us that at a certain time, on a certain day, every seven years, Manannán

MacLir, the great Celtic guardian of the sea, allows this island to be seen by people lucky enough to be in the right place at the right time. Its beauty enchants all those who see it, but no matter how hard they try, they are never able to reach its magical shores. But the sight of this island remains engraved in their minds for the rest of their lives.

The king of this magical place is Aengus, and his queen is Edain. It is said that only those chosen by their beautiful daughter, Princess Niamh of Tír na nÓg, can set foot upon this enchanted island. Over the centuries, only one man, Oisín, the warrior poet of the Fianna, is known to have visited and lived in Tír na nÓg, but unfortunately, he was lost to the ravages of time upon his return to Ireland. Niamh loved Oisín very much and was overwhelmed with loneliness when he failed to return. For centuries, she kept a lonely vigil watching out over the horizon wondering what had become of him. At the appointed time, every seven years, she went in search of him, but she was never able to find her long-lost love.

There the story of Niamh and Oisín might have ended, but for three children who made a magical journey to the Land of Eternal Youth. They were Luke Silke and Danielle Furey, both of whom were ten years old at the time, and David O'Brien, aged twelve. The children lived on Inishmaan, one of the Aran Islands which lie off the west coast of Ireland, close to Galway. Over the centuries, islanders and, indeed, visitors to the island have claimed they saw the fabled land of Tír na nÓg from the western shore of Inishmaan.

These children were destined to become part of folklore history after they went in search of adventure and became prisoners of time. This is their story, and the story of Niamh's quest.

Meeting Princess Niamh

One day, three friends, David, Danielle and Luke, were playing together on a beach on the western shore of the island of
Inishmaan. The day was warm and sunny with a slight haze hanging over the ocean. Through the children's laughter the sound of sea
birds and waves washing over the sand could be heard. The children
had been playing football for some time when Luke remembered
that he had to return home soon as he had left earlier that morning
without doing some jobs for his mother.

Suddenly an eerie silence fell over the beach, the seabirds
vanished and even the waves made no sound, as time and tide
seemed to stand still. The children froze and stared towards the
ocean, and as they watched a figure appeared out of the haze.

A huge white horse with silver shoes began to emerge and
galloped across the waves towards them. Although the children
were stunned, Luke managed to say in a low voice, 'The horse is
galloping on top of the sea.'

They watched carefully as the horse came closer. It was almost
moving in slow motion, with nostrils flaring and a long white mane
flowing behind him.

David and Danielle were frightened and wanted to run away.
They began pulling at Luke who was spellbound and could not
move. But it was too late; the horse was now almost upon them.
It stopped in front of the children, who were now mesmerised
by the vision before them. The rider of this magnificent animal

was a very beautiful young woman. Her long, almost golden hair hung loose down past her shoulders, reaching almost to her waist. Entwined in her hair on either side of her head were two long narrow-braided plaits that seemed to have streaks of silver running through them. Her delicate features and light tanned complexion gave her a look of elegance. She had deep-blue eyes like the ocean and wore a dark-blue silk cloak that was speckled with golden stars. The border of her purple dress was embroidered with floral and honeybee motifs. Her beauty captivated the children.

In a wonderful soft voice, the lady spoke to the stunned children. She told them not to be afraid and said that she was searching for a young man who rode a great chestnut-coloured horse. The children remained silent and open-mouthed before David bravely asked, 'Who are you?'

'I am Niamh Chinn Óir [Niamh of the Golden Hair].'

'Where have you come from?' Danielle asked.

'I come from a magical island called Tír na nÓg – a land far, far away, across the sea, where my father Aengus is king and my mother Edain is queen.'

The princess asked the children if they had ever seen or heard of a young horseman named Oisín who came riding out of the sea just as she had done.

They said no, and on hearing their reply a look of sadness appeared on Niamh's face.

Still fascinated, Luke asked, 'How did you ride on top of the water?'

'All things are possible in Tír na nÓg,' she replied.

Then, almost together, the children asked her why she was sad and who was the young horseman Oisín.

She said it was a long story, one that had begun many centuries before they were born. When they asked her how Oisín could still be alive after such a long time, Niamh told them that Tír na nÓg was a magical place where no one grows old or suffers illness. Like her, Oisín also rode a magical horse and could travel anywhere he wanted and would remain young, provided he remained on the horse.

The children asked her to join them on the beach and tell them the story of Oisín and Tír na nÓg. She refused to dismount from the magnificent horse, but began to tell her story.

Many years ago, she had come to Ireland to meet with Oisín, the warrior poet and son of the great Celtic chieftain, Fionn Mac Cumhail. Fionn was the leader of the Fianna, a brave band of ancient Irish warriors, and Oisín was their greatest poet. She told them how she had fallen in love with Oisín and how they had returned to Tír na nÓg together. Oisín became a great chieftain in her land and they remained happy and contented for a long, long time.

However, one day Oisín began feeling homesick and asked her if it were possible for him to return to Ireland, just to visit his family and friends.

Niamh told him that it was not as easy as it might seem to leave Tír na nÓg. The only person who could grant such a request was her father and, once it was granted, the magic of Tír na nÓg was transferred to the horse for the journey.

Having spoken with her father, Niamh told Oisín that he could indeed travel to Ireland, but that he must remain mounted on the magical horse at all times. If he dismounted, even for a second, then all the years that he had lived in Tír na nÓg would immediately come upon him, and he would age tremendously and die.

Oisín became concerned and asked her how long he had been in Tír na nÓg.

'How long do you think you have been here, Oisín?'

Knowing that this was an enchanted land, he paused for a moment and said, 'About three years.'

Niamh smiled sadly at him and said, 'You have been here at least three hundred years, Oisín.'

He was shocked at first, but then felt sure that she was mistaken.

Niamh accompanied Oisín to the ocean and kissed him good-bye, saying, 'Be careful, Oisín, and hurry back to me. I cannot imagine my life without you.'

Oisín told her that he loved her, and not to worry, that no matter what happened he would return before the third sunset. She was more important to him than all the treasures of the ancient world, and, with a smile, he turned and rode out onto the ocean.

Niamh watched, with her heart sinking in her chest, as he rode out to sea. She never saw him again because he did not return to Tír na nÓg as he had promised. She knew that something must have happened to him, as he would not have stayed away for so long.

All the people in her land believed that he must be dead, but Niamh loved Oisín so much that she never let those thoughts enter her mind. Instead, she believed that, somehow, Oisín was still alive.

'On the night before I set out on my quest, I went to the highest point of the headland, and there, while the waves rested on the shore, I sang a spirit-calling song out over the ocean to try and awaken the spirit of my beloved Oisín and let him know that I was coming to take him home. This is a ceremony that I have performed many times over the centuries and people who have heard my song believe it is the sound of a mermaid and, I am told, are enchanted by it. I will go on searching until I find him, or find out what became of him.'

'What will you do now that you cannot find Oisín?' asked Danielle in a kind voice.

'I will return to Tír na nÓg and set out on this quest another day,' Niamh replied sadly.

'Can we go back with you?' Luke suddenly blurted out, totally oblivious to Niamh's sadness.

David was more polite and asked if it were possible to travel with her to the Land of Eternal Youth. Danielle, who was entranced by Niamh's account of her love and loss, remained silent.

Niamh said that even though her horse was big and strong enough to carry all of them, it would be dangerous because if for any reason they dismounted and delayed any length of time in Tír na nÓg, they would never be able to return to their own time and place.

'Remember,' Niamh said, 'time stands almost completely still

in Tír na nÓg and you have no way of knowing how much time will pass in your own world while you are away. All that you know could disappear into the past if you remain there for too long. I can tell you more about Tír na nÓg. It is a beautiful and magical place and, as I have already told you, it is a land of eternal youth where people do not grow old and where the crops never fail. It is a land of luscious fruit trees and flowers, and the rain falls only at night or when the people wish it to do so.'

While she was talking, the children knew they would love to go to this magical land. When Niamh had finished speaking, Danielle asked excitedly if they could visit Tír na nÓg, even just for a short time, and return home without getting off the horse.

'Yes,' said Niamh, looking at their eager faces. She warned them again that they must be very careful and remain on the horse at all times. If they dismounted for any reason, then only her father could grant them permission to leave, as it was his magic that carried them above the waves.

Off to Tír na nÓg

Niamh leaned down and helped the children up onto the horse. Danielle and Luke sat in front of Niamh while David, who was older, sat behind her. She turned the horse to face the ocean and they were soon galloping out to sea. As David looked back, he could see the haze close behind them, blocking any view of Inishmaan.

The children were a bit frightened at first, but after a short time they got used to the movement of the horse. As they rode further out to sea a fishing boat loomed in the distance and, as they came closer, David recognised his father's boat. As they passed, David could see Gavin, one of his older brothers, a family friend and his father on board. Because they were looking in his general direction he expected to hear his father call out to him, but he remained silent.

'That's my dad's boat, but I don't think he sees me,' David said to Niamh.

Niamh then told them that once the horse began its journey across the sea they became invisible to all, except those living in the Land of Eternal Youth. Nevertheless, David still shouted to the boat and could see by the reaction of those on board that they had heard him but could not see him.

On the boat, Gavin told the others that he thought he had heard David shouting, but his father dismissed it as the screech of a seagull carried on the wind.

After some time, they began to see the vague outline of an island

on the horizon. It was shrouded in mist. As they came closer to the island the mist cleared and the children looked down into a clear, bright-blue sea. Suddenly, just beneath the waves, a beautiful girl with long, fair hair swam. They soon realised she had a fish-like tail that propelled her gracefully through the water.

'My God,' Danielle exclaimed, 'it's a mermaid!'

'Yes,' Niamh replied, 'they watch over our sea.'

The children were fascinated, but their attention was soon drawn to three men riding chestnut-coloured horses close by. Two of the men were young and were armed with swords of gold and silver; the third was much older, with long white hair and a beard. The older man was wearing a green robe and a red tunic inside. He carried an oval shield made of gold and bronze, which was inlaid with coloured glass and gemstones.

'Prepare yourselves for the Land of Eternal Youth,' Niamh said. Then in a whisper she told the children that the older man was the only unhappy person in Tír na nÓg.

They felt the thud of the horse's hooves as he galloped out of the sea and on to a beautiful, white, sun-drenched beach. There to meet them were a number of smiling horsemen wearing white and red clothing; some of them had blue cloaks, while others wore red and yellow. The leader carried a shield similar to the one that they had seen carried by the old man. It flashed in the sunlight, sending beautiful colours along the upwards-sloping strand.

'You are welcome home Niamh, and who are your young companions?' the leader asked as he urged his horse closer.

'Thank you, Gearóid. These are my friends from Ireland,' and she introduced the children. 'I have promised to show them our enchanted island before I take them home.'

'You are welcome to Tír na nÓg,' Gearóid said, smiling kindly at the children.

Niamh explained that Gearóid was one of her father's finest warriors, and that he always came to greet her upon her return.

As they rode up and over the headland of the beach they saw a lush green-forested landscape, with light-blue-grey mountains dotting the horizon. In the distance stood a magnificent white castle.

'That's my father's castle,' Niamh said.

David leaned out from behind Niamh to get a clearer view.

'Careful,' Niamh said suddenly. 'Remember my warning about not falling off the horse.'

David immediately clung harder to Niamh's cloak.

A great stone wall surrounded the castle. Hanging from its battlements were silk banners displaying all the colours of the rainbow. A huge elaborately carved archway led into the inner castle grounds.

'I will see you back at the castle later, Niamh,' Gearóid said.

'Yes, Gearóid,' Niamh replied, 'but I will be late as I have to return to Ireland with the children first.'

Gearóid and the other horsemen then left them and rode back along the beach.

'Where are they going, Niamh?' asked David.

'They are just exercising the horses. They will take them along the full length of the beach and around by the mountains before returning.'

A long and very wide avenue led to the decorated arch. It was lined on both sides with sycamore trees covered in rich foliage. Throughout the surrounding area there were many orchards, containing a large variety of fruit. Beyond the castle the lush, green landscape continued on to meet a wild forest and, beyond all of this, dazzling green and purple mountains seemed to touch the perfect blue sky.

Pointing to the right of the mountains, Niamh told the children that the water from the falls formed a beautiful crystal-clear river just beyond the forest, and it was this river that supplied the wells in Tír na nÓg with excellent drinking water.

A large number of people were gathered in front of the castle walls, and the children noticed that everyone seemed very friendly and happy. The men were dressed in colourful robes, the women wore garments of coloured silk, and all were smiling and strolling around without a care in the world.

'Why is everyone smiling?' asked David.

'Why not?' said Niamh. 'Our people are very happy here.'

The children also noticed that there were exotic birds of all descriptions moving throughout the orchards and grounds of the castle, giving off a stunning array of moving colour. There were sounds of delightful music as musicians played a variety of instruments, and young women dressed in beautifully coloured costumes, danced to the joyful sounds.

When they approached a long, glittering, silver drawbridge over a moat, the children were captivated by the sight of swans gliding by in pairs, not just gleaming white, but sets of black swans as well. They were fascinated as they came closer to the stone archway, on either side of which hung flowing rainbow banners.

The walls of the castle loomed before them, decorated with light-reflecting nuggets of white stone. They arrived before two great doors, each of which was decorated with twin gold panels that reflected the sunlight. A stone lion sat on either side of the great doors, guarding the entrance. The courtyard and front of the castle was paved with gleaming blue-grey cobblestones, which continued along a large wide path leading off on one side of the castle into a beautifully circular garden. In the centre of the garden stood a huge, white marble fountain decorated with lions and horses. Water gushed from the mouths of the animals, and miniature blue dolphins swam round and round in the fountain.

Brightly coloured flowers of all descriptions, shrubs and miniature trees lined the pathway as it surrounded the fountain and continued for some distance on the opposite side, giving way to another large, ornate archway. A similar fountain was beyond and as far as the children could make out, this pattern was repeated.

Gazing at the magical surroundings in which they now found themselves, the children were intensely excited. Danielle asked if they could meet Niamh's father, as she had never met a king before.

'Of course,' Niamh replied, and called out to her father, but received no answer.

She very carefully dismounted and held the horse by the reins, calling out to her father again. Still only silence greeted her. Niamh looked up at the children and asked David to take control of the reins for a moment while she went inside the castle to look for him.

Although Niamh was only gone for a short time, David became a little impatient. He turned the horse towards the drawbridge, and began to urge the animal forward. The others pleaded with him not to move, but he said, 'I just want to see those swans again. I'll be careful. Anyway, nothing bad can happen – we're in Tír na nÓg.'

As they passed beneath the archway, Luke leaned out to touch one of the coloured banners that was moving gently in a slight breeze, and he almost fell. To save himself he grabbed the banner, but it was not strong enough to support him and it fell down on top of them, frightening the horse and causing it to rear up on its hind legs.

The three of them fell to the ground and the horse ran quickly away. Luckily, none of them was hurt, but as they stood up, Luke began to blame David for urging the horse over the drawbridge. David immediately turned on him, saying that he should not have pulled down the banner.

Danielle, standing between both of them, said, 'We should try to go after the horse or find Niamh instead of arguing.'

By now, the horse was well out of sight, so they decided to go into the castle and find Niamh.

Journey to the Land of Silence

Just then, Niamh returned, and seeing the children on the ground she hurried towards them asking what had happened. Whilst she was relieved that none of them was injured, she was also a little worried as she realised that they now had to find her father as the children could be trapped in Tír na nÓg if something was not done. She ran to the drawbridge to see if she could catch sight of the horse, but there was no trace of him. As Niamh turned back, she heard Danielle ask, in a worried tone, if they would be able to get home?

Before she could answer, David attacked Luke, saying that it was all his fault, but Niamh pulled the boys apart and gathered the children around her, telling them not to worry, that she would find her father and he would help them to return home. When they asked why they could not leave immediately, Niamh reminded them that she needed her father's permission to leave Tír na nÓg, as the magical spell which enabled her to travel across the sea to Ireland had to have her father's blessing.

Niamh told the children to stay where they were and she ran back into the castle. She found one of the servants, who said that her father had gone to the Land of Silence.

They would have to follow him there, so Niamh checked the stables, but all of the horses were gone, which meant that they would have to walk. This worried her as it was a long way and it looked like the children would have to spend at least one night in Tír na nÓg.

She returned and explained to the children that her father had gone to the Land of Silence, a part of Tír na nÓg where people go to meditate and take total rest.

'We must stay together and follow him quickly. Go pick some fruit and eat before the journey.'

Niamh noticed the worried look on the children's faces and, although she was a little anxious herself, she did not wish to upset them, and reassured them by saying that if they hurried, then everything would turn out all right.

As the children were about to go and pick the fruit, they saw a beautiful lady coming towards them from the gardens. She was carrying flowers and she was wearing a white, flowing gown which had thin stripes of yellow and silver running the length of it. The gown was tied at the waist with a strip of pink fabric.

'Wait a moment, children, here is my mother,' said Niamh, and they greeted each other with a hug and kiss.

The children immediately noticed the strong resemblance that Niamh bore to her mother. They were very alike, just that the queen had silver streaks running through her long, light-brown hair, which added an air of nobility to her beautiful appearance.

'Who are these children, Niamh, and where have they come from?' the queen asked.

Niamh introduced the children to her mother. She smiled and spoke softly to each of them. After Niamh briefly explained to her mother what had happened, she said, 'We do not have much time. I must find Father quickly.'

The queen did not reply, but looked at the children again and, smiling, said, 'You may go to the orchards now to pick some fruit, children. I wish to speak to Niamh alone for a moment.'

They did not have to be asked twice, and ran towards the orchards.

'Your father will not be pleased, Niamh,' the queen said.

'I know, Mother, but we must go to him nonetheless,' Niamh replied.

'I know that you meant well by bringing the children here to see our country, but you must be more careful with your heart, Niamh – it is the cause of most of your problems. I will remain at the castle in case you miss your father on the journey.'

The children went from one orchard to another – some contained apples, pears, cherries and peaches and some had lemons, while others contained oranges – all gleaming in the sunshine. Luke ran to one of the peach trees and picked some fruit and, almost immediately, new fruit appeared. David and Danielle joined him and picked more fruit, and again the fruit reappeared.

Throughout the different orchards, people were harvesting the various fruits. Danielle noticed an older-looking lady who was picking fruit close by, and asked her how many orchards there were in Tír na nÓg.

'As many as we need. Once the fruit is taken, the tree immediately replaces it – it is part of the magic here.'

Luke then asked, rather cheekily, 'How come, if this is the Land of Eternal Youth, you look old?'

Danielle was embarrassed at Luke's remark, but the woman just smiled and told him that she was already old when she came to Tír na nÓg.

Niamh arrived in the orchard and told the children it was time to go and find her father. As they made their way through the courtyard at the rear of the castle, the children could not help but notice the very finely built horse stables on their right. The red half-doors gleamed as if only just freshly painted. Even the outhouses on the left were splendidly built. Once they reached the end of the courtyard, they set out along a wide, white, sandy pathway that made its way through the green pasture ahead.

'Where is the Land of Silence?' Danielle asked.

'Just to the left,' Niamh replied, pointing, 'beyond that mountain range.'

Niamh then told the children how she and Oisín had walked this path many times together, and as she spoke they noticed tears well up in her bright, glowing eyes.

Without saying anything, David and Danielle, who were walking on either side of Niamh, held out their hands to her, and the three of them walked together, while Luke ran ahead towards the forest. Niamh called out to him not to enter the forest alone.

Away off to the west, the children noticed beautiful multicoloured houses. Niamh said that they were not painted but were built of coloured stone. 'White, blue, green, yellow and many more coloured stones are quarried here in Tír na nÓg, and there are many similar villages throughout this enchanted land.'

Pointing to the east as they walked, Danielle asked what lay behind some low hills to the left of the snow-covered mountain range.

'Beyond the low hills the farms of Tír na nÓg are located.'

'What do they farm?' asked David.

'Many things, including dreams,' Niamh replied, smiling, as they continued to move forward.

'Why dreams?' asked Danielle.

'In these dreams, all your wishes come true and you can travel to wherever you desire. It is through dreams that many of our people can revisit their own past and the places they have lived without ever having to leave Tír na nÓg.'

'How do you farm dreams?' asked David.

'With the aid of dream catchers. In the morning all the dreams are collected and taken to that snow-capped mountain – it is called the Mountain of Dreams, and it is there that all dreams are stored until people wish to revisit them. There are thousands of dreams stored there.'

'Surely you could meet Oisín again by dreaming of him?' said Danielle.

'Of course I have taken this dream to the mountain, but remember that is the world of dreams and that is all they are – dreams. You must still wake up to reality every morning.'

On reaching the edge of the forest, Luke sat on a stone and rested while waiting for the others to arrive. When they reached him, Niamh warned the children not to stray from the stone-lined pathway as ancient spirits haunted the forest. Niamh noticed a worried look on the children's faces and quickly added,

'Provided you do not leave the pathway, no harm can come to you.'

They entered the forest together. Some of the trees stood straight up like needles, while others had branches shaped like distorted arms stretching out as if they were trying to grab at something or someone. It was dull in the forest as the sun was partly blocked out by the rich canopy of branches and leaves at the tree tops. However, shafts of sunlight penetrated down through the trees, giving the place a sense of magic and wonderment. Wild vegetation covered the forest floor and provided a haven for the little woodland creatures. Flowers were growing in some sections along the edge of the pathway, and Danielle asked if she could pick some.

'Of course,' Niamh replied. 'They will grow again immediately, just like the fruit.'

David Disappears

David had gone ahead of the others as he had a great interest in wildlife. When a fox wandered into his path, he ran towards it. The fox turned and disappeared into the undergrowth, and in his excitement David forgot Niamh's warning and followed it.

Niamh had not noticed David disappear into the forest, as she was busy helping Danielle pick flowers. Luke, who was behind Danielle and Niamh, did not see what had happened either, as he was trying to balance himself on the stones which lined the pathway.

David battled his way through bushes and briars, but lost sight of the fox. He turned to go back to the pathway, but he could not see it. Suddenly, the ground gave way beneath him, and as he called out for help, the earth swallowed him up.

The others, hearing him shout for help, scanned the forest immediately but could see no sign of him and did not even know the direction in which he had gone. Niamh warned the others not to leave the pathway under any circumstances and went looking for David.

She searched anxiously for him but dared not go too far into the overgrown forest for fear of getting lost. She returned to the pathway and, trying not to worry the children, told them that if they waited for a while, David would probably return.

They took turns in calling out to David, but the only reply was the rustle of the leaves in the tree tops. Niamh said they should find her father and seek his help first. It was now very late and the

forest was getting even darker, so she decided their best option was to shelter under a large nearby tree for the night and make a fresh start in the morning. In the meantime, David might even return.

Danielle and Luke were frightened and clung to each other, thinking of home and of the worry they must be causing their parents.

Earlier, on Inishmaan, David's mother, Jacqueline, was wondering why he had not come home for lunch. She waited another hour before making her way to the home of the Silkes and asked if he had been there. Luke's mother, Marita, said that she had not seen either of them since morning, adding that Luke should have come home as he had not done his jobs. While they were talking, Anna Furey arrived looking for Danielle. She had sent Danielle's younger sister Chloe to look for her earlier, but she could not find her. Anna told them that some of the other children said that they had seen the three of them together down on the beach, but that was some hours ago.

The three mothers became concerned and walked down to the beach together. There was no sign of any of the children, just David's ball floating in the water as the tide had made its way towards land and was washing against the headland. They began calling out to the children, but the only reply was the sound of the sea crashing against the land. David's mother waded out into the water and retrieved her son's ball, all the while looking out to sea. Her heart was sinking and tears welled up in her eyes and began to flow onto her cheeks as a horrible sense of fear overcame her. She turned and made her way back to the others and they went to raise the alarm.

By mid-afternoon the entire island had been searched for the missing children. Every available boat on the island and the two neighbouring islands had gone to sea to search for them, but as dusk arrived all the search parties were returning without having found any trace of them. Gavin, David's brother, swore that he heard David's voice call out that morning while they were out at sea, yet he could not understand how he had not seen him. The search was called off for the night, and a great sorrow hung over the families of the children, and indeed the people of the island, as they all made their way home.

Next morning, Niamh and the children resumed their search for David, but decided that it was better to go and find the king rather than waste any more time. They moved off quickly through the trees until they reached the other end of the forest. They soon arrived at the foot of the mountain range, which towered above them. Fantastic waterfalls cascaded down the mountain sides. They came to a wide stream, and crossed over a stone-carved humpback bridge, which gave access to the mountain paths. As they crossed the bridge, Niamh tried to hide her concern from the children, but they knew that she was worried about David. They did not fully understand her fear, as they thought Tír na nÓg was a beautiful place where nothing bad could happen. The Land of Silence lay beyond the mountains to the left. Niamh assured them that the climb would be easy as there were many paths leading to the top.

They seemed to be climbing forever and Danielle was getting tired, because while it was not a hard climb, it was certainly a long one. When they eventually reached the summit, they sat for a while and rested. Before them lay the most incredible views in all directions – it was hard to believe that such a land existed. Danielle and Luke looked back towards the forest and wondered again where

David might be. Niamh was looking in another direction down into the Land of Silence, which lay beneath them to the left.

'Come on, children. I can see movement in the land below.'

Before the children turned, Danielle had already noticed another lush green valley to the right of the mountain range. It was difficult to see clearly, but at the end of the valley Danielle could see a large rocky outcrop with a long, thin waterfall running down into a crystal-clear river. She watched as the river meandered its way through the valley, and, pointing, asked, 'What is that valley called?'

'That is the Land of the Lonely,' Niamh replied. 'Come on, children, we must hurry. And remember, you must remain silent at all times while you are in this land. Not even the wildlife makes noise here.'

'How will you tell your father that we are in trouble?' Luke asked.

'When my father sees me here with both of you, he will know immediately that something is wrong and return with us.'

It was mid-afternoon before they reached the bottom of the mountain, where a rolling and uneven landscape spread out before them. Various types of fruit trees grew throughout the land. There was also a large array of beautiful wild flowers, and berry-covered trees and shrubs growing all around. A most delightful fragrance hung in the air and Danielle was tempted to comment on it, but did not.

Luke, forgetting where he was, blurted out, 'What's that smell?'

'It's not me.' Danielle's face was flushed with embarrassment thinking that Luke did a 'rudey' and was trying to blame her, just like at school.

Luke laughed and was about to say something when Niamh quickly raised her finger to her lips and said, 'Shhh …'

It was too late. Their voices had already shattered the silence and seemed to carry for miles. A short time later people began to appear from all around, including Niamh's father.

As he walked towards them, the children got their first glimpse of a real king. He was dressed in a short scarlet tunic and blue trousers. The tunic was highly decorated with various motifs of the moon, sun and stars. Around his waist was a brown leather belt with a gold buckle and from it hung a gold-handled sword, its scabbard encrusted with coloured diamonds and gemstones. A long white cloak rimmed with embroidered designs hung from his shoulders. It reached down to his brown leather boots, just below the knees. He was a youngish looking man, not at all what the children had expected. His brown, shoulder-length hair and short beard had grey streaks running through them, making him even more distinguished looking. He looked curiously at the children first, then at Niamh and knew that he must return immediately.

David meets Cian

David woke up as an animal was licking his face, and forgetting where he was, he thought it was his little dog Minnie. Opening his eyes, he knew that it was not Minnie, but he was still not afraid because the animal was licking him. David looked around and thought he had landed at the bottom of some type of deep mineshaft. He realised that the tunnel where he found himself must have been man-made as it was lined on both sides and across the top with cut stones, while long stone lintels formed a roof.

But how could he know this? After all, he was below ground where it should be very dark. However, at the end of the tunnel ahead of him was the entrance to a cavern from which an eerie green light was being emitted. He raised himself up and began to walk slowly towards the entrance. The animal who was licking him was close by his side and, looking down, he saw it was the fox he had been chasing.

Once inside the cavern, he was astonished at its large size. He knew that it was also man-made as it was built with lavishly carved stones. David recognised the Celtic designs in the stones, as he had seen similar ones in his schoolbooks. There were large stone columns supporting the roof and all around the chamber were flat-topped stones on which one could sit. He looked across at a small hollow, about forty centimetres square, which was cut into the back wall of the chamber – it was from there the light was being emitted.

At first, he was a little afraid to move, but after a while he began

to approach it. As he got closer, he noticed that the light was coming from an object inserted in the mouth of a large, stone-carved head.

David stood for a moment before the head, observing that the eyes and mouth penetrated right through the stone as if there was a carved face on the opposite side also. The image facing him seemed young in appearance, and he wondered what the opposite side looked like. Gathering some courage, he removed the glowing object from the mouth. It was cool to the touch and felt like a stone. He immediately became aware of phantoms moving around, casting shadows across the walls of the chamber. The fox crouched close to the ground in fear and began to whimper. David was about to run away when a voice directly behind him whispered, 'Return the stone.'

He turned around quickly but there was no one there. He was

very frightened and immediately returned the stone; and then the phantoms disappeared.

He wondered just where he was and how he would find a way out. Returning to where he had fallen into the tunnel, David tried to climb up the shaft, but it was far too steep and high. He knew from looking up that the daylight was gone – it was definitely night-time. He shouted for help but no one came, and he began to wonder just how long he had been knocked out. He turned back towards the chamber, thinking there must be another way out, and noticed that the fox had disappeared.

David was very nervous upon entering the chamber the second time. He searched for another exit, but could not find any other way out. By now he was very tired so he lay down close to the cavern wall and, despite being frightened, fell asleep.

David awoke the following morning thinking that he had dreamt

it all, but very soon reality struck home as he realised that he was still in the chamber. Again he searched for a way out, but was disappointed once more. He sat for a while on one of the flat stones, thinking about what he should do next. Would he ever be able to return home? Where was Niamh? He began to panic, looked at the green stone again, and some of his courage returned, so he decided to risk moving it. As he took away the stone, the phantoms began to move around the chamber again, this time coming closer and closer to him. The whispers were becoming more frequent and were growing much louder.

David suddenly shouted out in fear and a little anger: 'Help me, I'm trapped!'

Suddenly, everything went quiet and the phantoms again retreated even though he had not returned the stone. Just as he was about to do so, movement at one end of the chamber distracted him. It was the fox.

'You got me in here, so you get me out,' David said to the fox.

As he spoke, he saw that the animal was becoming alarmed over something. He walked slowly towards the fox, who was now barking at an extremely large stone inserted in the wall of the chamber.

A face began to emerge from the stone, then hands and shoulders, and soon a strange and ancient-looking figure was standing in front of him.

David was terrified. The eyes of the apparition suddenly opened and looked directly at him,

'Why have you come here?' the strange figure asked.

David could not answer.

'You have disturbed our sleep by removing the green Stone of Envy.'

'I'm sorry,' David said, 'but I'm trapped and cannot escape

from this place. I miss my family and friends and I just want to go home.'

'Where do you come from?'

'Ireland,' David replied.

'Ireland …' the figure said, thoughtfully, 'that was my home in ancient times.'

'What type of creature are you?' asked David, before realising that he might have insulted the figure.

'I am no creature. I am Cian of the ancient Tuatha Dé Danaan of Ireland. How did you get into this chamber?'

David said that he had fallen through an opening in the earth.

'The exit once made by the Morrigan,' said Cian.

Becoming more comfortable with his surroundings, and gaining more courage, David asked, 'How did you get here?'

Cian then told David that after many years of his people ruling

Ireland, the country was invaded by the Celts and a great war broke out with the Tuatha Dé Danaan. 'My people were eventually forced into a treaty by the invaders and the Dé Danaan then took refuge in the underground passages of Ireland. The entrance to our world is located within the old ring forts of Ireland. Today you know my people as the fairies. Our king is Finvara, and his palace is located beneath the hill of Knock Ma, on the mainland of Ireland many miles from here.'

'I know the place,' David said, adding, 'I have visited it a number of times, but I never saw Finvara or his palace.'

'Oh it's there all right, and so is he, believe me,' said Cian. He then told David that the spirits of the Dé Danaan who were killed in the war were asked by the Morrigan if they wished to be taken to the House of Donn.

'Who is the Morrigan?' David asked. 'And where is the House of Donn?'

Cain then explained that the Morrigan was the goddess of battles. He told him that she was very powerful and could shape-shift and take on the appearance of various animals, including that of a crow.

'The House of Donn is located on an island off the south-west coast of Ireland. This is where all dead heroes feast and celebrate with Donn, the Celtic guardian of the dead, before they take their final journey to the "Otherworld". The spirits of my people asked her if she could take them to Tír na nÓg instead, where they could remain suspended in time and remember their great days of glory. They also requested that my spirit accompany them to this place and act as their protector. The Morrigan agreed but said that the spirits of the Dé Danaan would have to remain underground as phantoms and that my spirit should be encased in stone to protect the entrance.'

David listened intently to Cian and as soon as he finished he blurted out, 'Why are you encased in stone? What is the green Stone of Envy?'

'Slow down, one question at a time. Listen, and I will tell you all that happened in those ancient times. The sons of Tureen, the sworn enemies of the Dé Danaan, murdered me. They used stones to take my life and, in doing so, my blood became absorbed in stone, as did my spirit and I became one with the stone spirit. I am now the guardian of this secret place.

'The green stone that you question me about is part of a magical object that the Tuatha Dé Danaan brought with them to Ireland when they first arrived. It is the Stone of Destiny at Tara, the stone on which all Irish high kings were crowned. The Stone of Destiny would cry out in anger if an unlawful king sat on it. Only a true king could be crowned upon the stone. It stood at Tara for hundreds of years and when the Morrigan was about to take us to Tír na nÓg, I asked if we could take a small portion of our ancient magical stone with us in memory of our glorious past, and she agreed.

'She then delivered our spirits here. It seemed impossible that such a dark place could exist in such a delightful, bright land as Tír na nÓg. Envy of the beautiful world, that exists above ground, seeped through our ranks and the Morrigan, realising that we may at some time wander from this dark place, struck the stone, making it glow green. She then announced that from that day forward it would be called the Stone of Envy and while it lights this place our sprits will rest. However, she then added a curse; that if anyone removed the stone and did not return it to its rightful place within three days, we would all disappear as if we never existed.

'The carved head in which it rests is the Janus Stone. It has two faces and was given to us by Janus, the guardian of time, and through its power we can remember our wonderful days in Ireland. This stone cannot be removed from this place either or it could cause a severe crisis, but there is no need for you to know about this right now.'

'If you are the guardian of this place, surely you can set me free,' David said.

'Yes,' said Cian, 'but first you must return the stone.'

David turned and was shocked to see that a ghost-like phantom now occupied each stone seat, and they were no longer mere phantoms, but were becoming more and more visible, taking on the appearance of ancient warriors.

'You must return the stone or their sprits will search for a way to the world above ground and wander like ghosts until they fade away into nothingness.'

David returned the stone quickly and, as he walked back towards Cian, the phantoms began to fade and disappear. Cian was also fading back into the stone. David ran towards him, but it was too late – he was gone.

He was about to cry out in anger when he heard a whisper: 'Fear not, I am Cian the honourable chieftain of an ancient race of Ireland, and I will secure your release.'

Just then, the large stone into which Cian had faded began to move and slide to one side and soon David and the fox were walking up through a tunnel of wild vegetation towards the daylight. They emerged into a lush green valley. The sunlight was very bright, causing David to squint and cover his eyes for a few moments. When his eyes became accustomed to the daylight, he looked around to see his surroundings. Ahead of him, he saw a large rocky outcrop high on a mountain. It was very far away at the other end of the valley. He could see a waterfall tumbling down from the outcrop into the crystal-clear river that was running through the valley. He looked back and saw a high cliff face in front of which there were many trees and brambles growing. To his right there was a mountain range, and the river ran to his left. David was unsure of which way to go and, turning around again, he decided to follow the fox who was making his way towards the other end of the valley, turning to look back every now and then as if to check that David was still behind him.

Return to the Castle

When they reached the crest of the mountain, Niamh introduced the children to her father and told him what had happened. He asked her how long they had been in Tír na nÓg and when she told him he said, 'You should not have brought them here, Niamh. We must get them back as soon as possible.'

Niamh hung her head a little and explained that she had expected to return to Ireland without even dismounting from the horse. Luke and Danielle defended Niamh, saying that it was also their fault as they had pleaded with her to take them to Tír na nÓg for a visit. What had happened with the horse was an accident.

'We will speak of this again. We need to act urgently and do not have time to look for your friend right now; we must get you home first,' said the king.

Luke and Danielle protested, saying that they could not return to Inishmaan without David.

But the king insisted, 'You must go now before any more time is wasted.'

By the time they reached the forest at the foot of the mountain it was getting dark, so they decided to spend another night sleeping under the trees, but not before calling out to David; there was no reply. That night the children again thought of home and the worry they must be causing their parents. How were they going to explain being gone for two nights?

Early the following morning, they began their journey back to the castle. The return journey seemed shorter, and they reached the castle by midday. When they entered the courtyard at the rear of the castle, the king walked to the stables. Gearóid and the others had also returned and there were a number of horses in the stables, including the great white horse that had taken them to Tír na nÓg. The children were a little surprised to see the animal in the stable. The king saw their reaction and said, 'The horse always returns after a time.'

He called out to some of his men and told them to saddle his horse and get him ready for the trip back to Ireland. He turned to the children and said, 'Now we must get you something to eat before your journey home.'

Niamh and the children, who were hungry by now, followed the king across the courtyard and through an archway leading to the front of the castle. They walked up the steps and entered through the great doors. Although they were extremely lonely and worried about David, Danielle and Luke stood in amazement once inside the castle doors. Before them lay numerous brightly coloured rugs spread across a black marble floor, encrusted with seashells of various colours, which had to be millions of years old. Huge white marble columns decorated with multicoloured flowers supported the white plastered ceiling. Strange and wonderful creatures peeped down at the children from the top of these columns and, indeed, from every corner of the building.

A great staircase swept up through the centre of the castle leading to the upper chambers. Two very real-looking stone unicorns guarded the stairway, one on each side. Large paintings of Celtic-like warriors decorated the walls of the castle. Open doors, on either side of where the children stood, led to large rooms that contained treasures that were even more beautiful. One room contained rows of large bookcases filled with books. In the other room, there was a very long banquet table, which was lined on

each side with fantastically carved chairs. In the centre of the table stood a silver candelabra complete with gold-coloured candles. A vase of flowers stood on each side of the candelabra.

'Come children, let us sit and eat,' said the king, and they all joined him at the table, which was already laid out with an abundance of their favourite foods.

Luke and Danielle looked at their plates. Danielle had corned beef, potatoes and mushy peas, while Luke tucked into shepherd's pie and, before they could ask, Niamh said, 'That's another part of the magic here, we know what people like to eat. Now eat up and we'll soon be on our way back to Ireland.'

Just then the queen entered the room. She walked over to the king and kissing him gently on the cheek said, 'You are welcome home, Aengus.'

Turning to the children, she said, 'Enjoy your food, children; you will soon be going home.'

It was only then she realised that one of them was missing. 'Where is the other boy?' she asked, directing the question at Niamh.

Before she could reply, the king interrupted, saying, 'Sit and join us, Edain, and we will explain the situation.'

After they had eaten, the children asked if they could take another look at the stables before going home.

'Of course,' said the king. 'Niamh and I will join you shortly.'

When the children had gone, her father spoke to Niamh. He told her that she must give up this quest for Oisín, that he must surely be dead by now and reminded her that hundreds of years had passed since he left Tír na nÓg.

Although Niamh's mother did not fully agree with her husband, she remained silent. Niamh was hurt by her father's words, but had to agree with him.

'If only I knew why he did not return or what happened to him,' she said.

'Perhaps you will never know. Did you ever think about Gearóid? He is one of my greatest warriors – he loves you, Niamh, and would always look after you.'

'Father,' she said, 'Gearóid is a good friend, and that is all he can ever be. While there is hope for Oisín, no matter how little, I can never think of anyone else. Please do not mention this again.'

Just then, there was a noise from the hallway outside and the king called out, 'Who's there?'

When there was no reply, he rose from the table and went to investigate, but as he crossed the room, he heard the castle doors slam shut.

'It must have been one of the servants closing the door after the children.'

Turning back to Niamh he asked, 'Did you tell the children why they must leave Tír na nÓg before sunset today?'

'No,' replied Niamh, 'I did not wish to frighten them.'

'Well, maybe you should have – if they have not left by sunset on the third day of their visit, then the three days will immediately become fifty years in Ireland.'

'That will not be a problem,' Niamh said. 'I will leave with them within the hour and have them home well before sunset.'

'You must stay with the children until you have located their families and reassure them that David will be found and well looked after here in Tír na nÓg. You must explain what has happened and, most importantly, that when he is found, why he cannot return to his own time. Sadly, Tír na nÓg will no longer be a place of wonder and mystery, but rather a place that people will fear. As soon as you are on the way, we will begin the search for David.'

Niamh then left to go and join the children.

'You do not agree with my words, Edain,' the king said.

'No, Aengus, not with all you have said, but I do agree that something must have happened to Oisín, as he would never have left Niamh. You must understand, Aengus, that Niamh truly loves Oisín and, God help her, she cannot stop loving him. I know her heart – it would have been the same for me.'

The king was about to say something, but she quickly added, 'Please listen to me for a moment, Aengus. Think about how we met all those centuries ago when I went to those islands where an ancient fort still bears your name. We fell in love and you were enchanted away to this kingdom. Our love has not diminished with time. Our story is very similar to their story, except without the tragedy.

'Apart from the loss of Oisín, the plight of the children will have an even worse affect on Niamh. I fully understand that it was foolish of her to bring them here, but she did it for all the right reasons. She is very much aware of this herself and will find it extremely difficult to come to terms with her own actions.'

The king then said, 'I do understand and feel great sympathy for Niamh, but I cannot excuse what has happened. I had to say something to try to bring her to her senses, Edain. I too miss Oisín, not like Niamh of course, but he was like a son to me. He was my greatest warrior and would have eventually ruled over this land. We will speak no more of this for now. I must organise the search for the missing boy and see that the other children leave for home immediately.'

Running Away

When Danielle and Luke reached the stable, the horse was already saddled and ready to go. Danielle turned to Luke and said, 'Luke, I don't want to go home without David.'

'Neither do I,' he replied.

'We could go back and look for him ourselves,' she said.

'We should wait for Niamh and her father,' David replied.

'No,' said Danielle, 'they will only insist on us going home without him. What harm can it do to stay another day; we're already in big trouble at home, aren't we, and we will be in bigger trouble if we return without David.'

'OK,' replied Luke. 'This is where all your riding lessons will come in handy.'

He helped Danielle up onto the horse, and then climbed up behind her. Once they were both mounted, Danielle urged the horse towards the stable doors and out into the courtyard. There was no one in sight. She turned the horse towards the archway leading to the forest road. As soon as they were out of the courtyard, they galloped back towards the huge forest.

When Niamh went to the stable and discovered that the children and the horse were missing, her heart sank as she feared for their safety. She ran back towards the castle, shouting, 'Father, Father, the children have gone.'

Her father met her with outstretched arms as she ran up the steps. 'What is the matter, Niamh?'

Almost breathless, she blurted out, 'The children have gone.'

'Where to?'

'I don't know, I don't know. I just know that they have gone.'

Before she could say another word, her father said, 'I know where. They have gone back to look for their friend.'

He called out urgently to Gearóid and his men and they came running into the castle grounds. 'Saddle your horses immediately. The children have gone back to the forest to look for their missing friend. We must find them before sunset as this will be their third day in Tír na nÓg and we all know what that means.'

Once the children reached the forest, they began calling out to David, but there was no reply.

'Danielle, we must hurry,' said Luke. 'Niamh and her father

will have missed us by now and I am sure they are already on the way to take us back. Anyway, if David was still in the woods we would have found him by now. He must have moved on.'

'Yes,' replied Danielle, 'but which way would he have gone?'

'Well, he definitely didn't return to the castle, or we would have met up with him. He must have gone towards the mountains, so we better keep moving in that direction.'

The king and the others were riding in hot pursuit. An over-whelming sense of panic, guilt and worry was clutching at Niamh as they rode towards the forest. She knew in her heart that it would be extremely difficult to locate the children and have them out of Tír na nÓg before sunset, as it was already afternoon, but they had to try.

It was late afternoon when Danielle and Luke reached the far side of the forest. They crossed the bridge and scanned the moun-tain paths looking for any sign of David. They called out to him again and again, but there was nothing to be seen, or no reply – just the sound of water running down the mountain.

They were overcome with tiredness and decided to spend the night there, rather than risk getting lost in the mountains. Before falling asleep, the children spoke of home and Luke was thinking of what excuses they were going to have to make up to account for their absence. After all, no one would believe them if they said that they had been to Tír na nÓg.

They found some shelter under a tree and cuddled up close to each other for warmth and comfort. Some time later, they were awakened by the sound of horses. Rubbing his eyes, Luke said, 'They have caught up with us.'

The king, followed by Niamh and his men, soon emerged from

the forest. He was angry at first, as they had disobeyed his orders, but he soon realised that the children had no idea of the consequences of their actions.

How was he going to tell them that by morning, fifty human years would have passed in Ireland? He knew that he should have warned them himself while they were at the castle, but how was he going to tell them now?

Niamh was gripped by guilt for placing the children's lives at risk and before the king could say anything she told the children to come closer as she had something very important to tell them.

She sat on a large stone in front of Luke and Danielle and put her arms around them as they knelt down. She hugged them and tried to reassure them at first by telling them that she would always look after them.

They were confused and a little worried at Niamh's words and began to ask her why she was saying this – after all, they were definitely going home in the morning.

'Do you remember the story of Oisín, and how when he returned to Ireland, a great many years had passed?'

They looked up into Niamh's face and nodded.

'Well,' said Niamh, 'every year in Tír na nÓg is equal to one hundred years in Ireland.'

Before she could go on, Luke was doing his sums.

'But we have only been three days in Tír na nÓg,' he said.

'That is correct,' said Niamh. 'But the problem is, if you stay in Tír na nÓg past three sunsets, it immediately becomes fifty human years. I did not want to tell you all along, as you may have been frightened. It is completely my fault that you are in this dreadful situation. We can return to Ireland tomorrow, but everything will have changed.' As she spoke, Niamh was also thinking that their families and friends might have died or moved away, but she did not want to alarm them any more than she had already.

They were stunned into silence and disbelief and tears began running down Danielle's face. She could not think of anything but her mum and dad. Would they still be there? And what of little Chloe?

Luke was having similar thoughts and with tears welling up in his eyes, he said, 'I still want to go home.'

Niamh again pulled both children into her arms and hugged them tightly, and Danielle, sobbing through her tears, said that she too wanted to go home. Thoughts of never seeing their families again shot through their confused young minds. They were both crying; they had never felt so alone or so afraid. Niamh hugged them even tighter.

The king remained silent for the most part, but reassured them that they would always have a good home in Tír na nÓg if they wished to stay.

They did not reply.

Return to Inishmaan

It was a restless and almost sleepless night for all of them; the children hardly spoke a word. The following morning they made their way back to the castle. Luke and Danielle still could not come to terms with what Niamh had told them. Perhaps they were dreaming, or she could be wrong – how could fifty years pass so quickly, they were wondering?

Niamh and her father rode side by side for most of the journey, with the others following behind. He warned her not to let the children dismount when they reached Ireland.

'I feel great sorrow for them,' he said, 'but there is nothing I can do but allow them to see their homeland. They will not fully believe or realise what has happened until they see the changes that will have taken place while they were away. I feel that they may wish to return to Tír na nÓg once they come to terms with what has happened, so do not let them dismount under any circumstances as they will lose all of their youth and join any surviving family members in old age.'

Niamh agreed and stayed silent for the remainder of the journey. She was thinking about her actions, and her guilt was overwhelming.

When they arrived back at the castle, the king issued orders to his men to escort the children and Niamh to the sea. Niamh would return with the children to their homeland while the king and the remainder of his men went again in search of David.

Once they reached the beach, Niamh and the children set out

across the ocean. This time there was an eerie silence as all of them were thinking about David being left behind and, of course, they feared what might await them on Inishmaan.

Could it all be really true, Luke wondered.

On the horizon, an island appeared before them. Luke broke the silence by uttering the word 'Home'. Soon their horse was striding across the shore at Inishmaan, where only a few short days ago they had met Niamh. How their lives had changed so much since that encounter. Everything was quiet as they crossed the headland reaching a small road leading across the island. Everything looked much the same and it looked like there was nothing to worry about, Luke thought to himself. He was about to jump from the horse when Niamh stopped him, saying, 'We will ride to your homes first, Luke, or at least try and find your family.'

As they rode up onto the road, Niamh noticed an old-looking man leaning on the wall of a small stone enclosure on a hill overlooking the sea. They rode up the long, narrow road to reach the little enclosure. As they drew closer an old and wrinkled face turned to them in astonishment and greeted them with a smile.

'Where did you come from?' asked the man, squinting as he looked up at the strange riders that had just emerged from the seashore.

'I will tell you later,' Niamh replied, and asked after the Furey, Silke and O'Brien families.

The man looked at her strangely, and answered, 'All gone except for me.'

'And who are you?' asked Luke.

'I am Gavin O'Brien,' replied the man, who was now even more curious.

Luke and Danielle, who were mounted in front of Niamh,

did not recognise the man even though he had been a childhood friend. After a few minutes they realised who he was and they became upset. Niamh leaned forward to comfort them.

'It's strange, but I feel as if I know these children!' the man said to Niamh.

'My name is Luke Silke,' and 'I'm Danielle Furey, and this island is our home!' the children blurted out almost together. They tried to explain to Gavin that they had left Ireland only four days ago to visit Tír na nÓg with Niamh, but were delayed because they had lost their friend David O'Brien and did not want to return home without him.

Both were talking so fast that they were confusing the man.

When Niamh confirmed their story, the man was astonished. The colour drained from his face and he grabbed hold of the horse by the reins, crying out, 'I don't believe this is happening to me. You're not real. You're all dead – disappeared many years ago when we were all children.'

Niamh leaned over and touched Gavin's shoulder, saying in a soft, kind voice, 'We are real.'

Before she could say anything else, he shouted at them as if they were playing some kind of nasty trick, saying, 'If you are real, then where is my brother David?'

He began to weep and as the tears ran down his weather-beaten face, he looked up again, his eyes focused on the young boy and girl seated on the horse. 'My God,' he exclaimed, 'it is ye. Have ye returned from the dead?'

'No, not the dead,' Danielle answered through her own tears. 'We're back from Tír na nÓg.'

Then she asked of her family and Gavin told her, 'They went to live on the mainland after the children – after you – disappeared. Your parents and mine have all passed away.'

Luke's face was white. He was lost for words for the first time in his life, but Gavin knew what he was thinking, and said, 'The same is true of your family, Luke.'

'My family also moved away,' Gavin told them, 'but I returned to fish the west coast and eventually settled here again. Your disappearance devastated all our families and, indeed, many of the islanders. I have never forgotten that day; it is embedded in my mind. I was always sure that I heard David call out to me while I worked on my father's boat.'

'You did,' Danielle said immediately. 'We saw you on our way to Tír na nÓg and David called out to you.'

Gavin looked up at the sky and said, 'I always believed that it was a sign that something had happened to David and to all of you. I never forgot any of you. Even in my dreams you come to visit me from time to time, but David … David has haunted me all these years.

'Please, this is all too much. Am I dreaming?' But he did not give them time to answer. 'Tell me what has become of David and why has he not returned with you?'

Not wanting to worry him any more then they had to, Niamh explained and reassured him that David was safe in the Land of the Young.

Gavin then asked what had happened to them and how and why had they caused so much worry and heartbreak for everyone.

As he spoke, the reality of their plight now hit Danielle and Luke – if they remained in Ireland, they would do so as old people, having missed the last fifty years of their lives. How they wished they could turn back the clock and return to their own lives.

They did not answer Gavin, so Niamh explained all that had happened since she met the children, saying that it was her quest to find Oisín that had caused all their troubles.

Oisín, the Last of the Fianna

'I have heard of Tír na nÓg and Oisín and the Fianna many times. They are age-old Irish fables handed down through generations of storytellers,' Gavin said.

Niamh asked him to tell her the story of what happened to Oisín after he returned to Ireland.

He looked up at her and said that it was a sad story – Oisín had arrived in Ireland hundreds of years ago, just a few miles from where he had first set out on his journey to Tír na nÓg. He searched all the main hunting grounds of the Fianna, but failed to find any of them. He went to the ancestral home of the Fianna also, but still no trace of them could be found. The once great ramparts of their forts were destroyed and overgrown with wild vegetation and brambles.

Oisín called out the names of his father and friends in anguish, but everything remained silent except for the echo of his own voice across the mountains, valleys and forests. He turned his horse and rode to another area where he knew the Fianna had often rested while on hunting expeditions, but again there was no trace of his family or friends.

After two days of fruitless searching, he decided to return to Tír na nÓg. According to the legend, it was while riding along the shore that Oisín saw some men struggling to move some large stones. He rode over to them and with some difficulty explained who he was, and told them that he was trying to find Fionn and the Fianna.

When they realised that he was really Oisín, they were astonished and told him that Fionn and the Fianna had all died long ago, many of them killed in ancient battles, and that they were now only part of ancient legends.

Shocked and upset, Oisín turned his horse hard to ride away and such was the force of the turn that the girth of the saddle broke and he fell on to the beach.

'This is the story that I was told, but other people say that he forgot Niamh's warning and jumped off the horse to help the men move the huge stones. Whatever the truth, once on the ground his features began to change and he aged quickly, his nails grew long, his hair turned white, his fine clothing turned to dust. His eyes reddened and misted over, and all the centuries he had spent in Tír na nÓg came upon him, ageing him by several hundred years. The men looked on in bewilderment and fright.

'Then one man ran away, calling, "Patrick! Patrick!"

'Patrick was a preacher who was travelling the countryside converting the people of Ireland to Christianity.

'The preacher rushed over to them and immediately tried to help Oisín. He took him into his care, but saw that Oisín was dying of old age. Patrick, who later became the national saint of Ireland, asked him who he was and where he had come from.

'As Oisín spoke, Patrick began writing down all the stories that Oisín told him of ancient times in Ireland, of Tír na nÓg and, of course, you Niamh. A short time later, Oisín died – he was the last of the great Fianna.'

Niamh listened intently to every word that Gavin uttered and as he came to the end of the story, tears welled up in her eyes and began streaming down her face as she said in a low, sad voice, 'I will never see my Oisín again.'

In her heart, Niamh had always known that something bad

had happened to Oisín, otherwise he would have returned to her. Her love for him had extended beyond centuries, but now she must let him go.

She gathered her thoughts and said to the children that they should return with her to Tír na nÓg.

Gavin looked up sadly at his childhood friends and agreed that it was the only thing they could do, adding that this island was no longer part of their world.

Luke and Danielle were very distressed as they would never see their parents again, and they would live out an eternity without their families in a place that was not their real home.

When they said this, Niamh was about to speak, but Gavin interrupted, saying, 'I am so sorry that this has happened to you, but nothing can be done now. I am sure Niamh is equally sad about what has happened and if there was anything that could be done to change things, she would do it. I know she will look after you wherever you are, and perhaps, in time, you will become accustomed to your new home.'

He then asked them to let David know that he had never forgotten him and would now live out the remainder of his life with some degree of contentment in the knowledge that he was alive and safe.

Gavin then said to Danielle. 'I will contact Chloe on the mainland and let her know that you are alive and well too, but I don't know how I will convince her that my story is true and not the ramblings of an old man gone mad with grief.

Turning to Luke he added, 'I will get word to your brother and sisters also Luke.'

Niamh and the children then reluctantly said their goodbyes to Gavin. They turned the horse towards the road leading down to the sea and with deep sadness in their hearts rode back to Tír na nÓg.

Throughout the journey, Niamh was full of mixed emotions – sadness, guilt and anxiety – because of the situation that the children were now in, and because of her thoughts of Oisín. For centuries she had lived in the hope of some day finding him and of them both returning to Tír na nÓg together where they would live forever in complete happiness. The plight of the children was the only thing that kept her going, and it also helped ease the terrible sense of personal sadness that she now felt – knowing she would never see her beloved Oisín again.

Search for David

When they arrived at her father's castle, Niamh and the children dismounted and were greeted by the queen. She told them that the king and some of his warriors had already gone in search of David and that they must follow. She then asked how they were received on Inishmaan and about the families of the children.

Niamh explained the situation briefly and then said, 'We must join the search for David, Mother. I will explain in more detail upon my return.' Turning to the children, she said, 'I will have another two horses saddled and we will ride separately. We will be faster and have more comfort – is that all right with both of you?'

It was no problem for Danielle as she was well able to ride. Luke felt confident because he had been on horseback so often over the past few days. Niamh then called on some of her father's men to have two horses prepared and ready for the children to ride.

The horses were in the stables and after Niamh helped Luke and Danielle to mount up, she jumped on her own horse and all three rode out of the courtyard towards the forest. They did not stop when they reached the forest, but rode straight through, calling out for David and the others as they went. They rode across the bridge, continued up the well-worn mountain trail, and did not stop until they reached the flat summit. Just then, a number of riders came towards them – it was the king and his warriors.

Niamh immediately asked if they had seen any sign of David.

'No, we have searched the forest and rode to the very extremities of the Land of Silence.' Turning to the children, he said, 'You are welcome back, children. We will take good care of you here.'

The children remained silent; the loneliness and pain they felt was overwhelming and they were fighting back their tears. They were terrified of the future without their parents; they wanted to scream and shout at Niamh, but did not, as they knew that they had caused some of the problems themselves, and that Niamh would do everything in her power to help them.

Niamh dismounted and told the king of the changes in Ireland, of how they had met Gavin O'Brien and how it was affecting the children.

'I know now what became of Oisín,' she then said.

There was a long silence as the king dismounted and listened to Niamh's story. After she finished, Niamh asked, 'Can anything be done father? Is there any way to turn back time? I'm not just thinking of Oisín, but I feel so responsible for the children's predicament.'

While they were talking, Danielle rode away from the others a small distance across part of the mountain range. She was thinking that maybe she should go to the Land of the Lonely, as this was how she was feeling. Looking from a high ridge, she saw a lone figure walking through the pasture below. Suddenly, the loneliness left her for a moment and she became very excited. Turning, she shouted to the others, 'It's David! I think it's David – he's in the valley below.'

The king jumped up.

'What is the matter with Danielle?' he called out to one of his men.

'I think she has just seen her friend,' one of them replied.

'Well, what are you all waiting for? Let's go,' he said as he mounted his horse, followed closely by Niamh.

Danielle did not wait for them. She turned her horse and urged the animal forward towards a nearby path and began to ride down the sloped mountain trail. The others lost no time and quickly followed her. She reached the pasture in good time, riding like the wind – so fast that her long dark hair stretched almost straight back with the speed of the horse. The horse galloped faster and faster over the rolling landscape, with the others close behind, straining to keep up.

The sound of the river was pleasing to David as he walked along, alone except for the fox, which was now far ahead of him. He had spent three nights sleeping under the stars, but he felt no fear, just extreme loneliness. The fruit trees provided an abundance of food. He was lost in his thoughts of Cian and all that had happened since he left home. He was thinking of his mum, dad and brothers, and of the last time he saw Gavin. 'Will I ever get home?' he wondered aloud.

Suddenly his thoughts were interrupted as the silence of the landscape began to shatter with the sound of galloping horses. Louder and louder until it sounded like thunder.

Turning around, a little startled, he saw Danielle charging forward towards him, with the others not far behind her. Before he could shout anything, Danielle was upon him, the animal's nostrils snorting noisily.

Danielle jumped off the horse, asking David what had happened to him. Before he could answer, the others arrived and all were dismounting fast, except for the king, who continued to ride on, unnoticed by the others.

Niamh grabbed David by the shoulders and asked if he was well. Before David could answer any questions, Danielle and Luke blurted out how they had returned to Ireland only to find that many years had passed and that Gavin was now an old man.

They explained all that had happened since they last saw him, and when they gave him Gavin's message he became very upset.

'We're trapped. I'll never see my family again,' he said.

Danielle and Luke nodded and again asked David where he had been.

He remained silent, just staring at the ground.

Luke was angry and shouted at him, 'It's all your fault we're trapped here. If you hadn't run away we would not have wasted so much time looking for you and we'd be at home. Now you won't even tell us where you were hiding.'

David lost his temper and ran at Luke, attacking him. Niamh and Gearóid grabbed the boys and separated them.

Niamh held David back and looking at Luke, said, 'That's

unfair Luke. I am the cause of your problems, not David. I should not have brought you here in the first place.' Putting her arm around Luke's shoulders, she added, 'Give my father time. I am sure he will think of something.'

She only then realised that he was not present – he had ridden on deeper into the Land of the Lonely.

Brasil's Story

Just as they were about to mount their horses, King Aengus appeared on the brow of a hill some distance away.

'Wait, my father is returning,' said Niamh.

As they looked towards the hill, they could see that he was not alone – behind him were three other riders. As they came closer, the children immediately recognised them: they were the men that they had seen riding on the ocean when they first arrived in Tír na nÓg. The old man with the long white hair and beard was again flanked on either side by the two younger men.

When they reached Niamh and the children they all dismounted and sat by the river. The king was about to introduce his companions, but before anyone could say anything, Luke looked at the old man and asked, 'Who are you?'

There was silence for a few moments and then he answered, 'I am Brasil, an ancient chieftain of Ireland.'

'How come you live here?'

'The king has told me of your plight, so now I will tell you my story. I once ruled a land across the sea called Connacht, in the western part of Ireland. My home was a large ringfort on the banks of the river Corrib. It was called Dangan and I held that place secure from all invaders. Its underground passages ran for miles, and made it very difficult for any enemy to follow. It was the last place of refuge against many powerful adversaries and even today it still holds its ancient magic.'

'Is that in Galway?' Luke asked.

'Yes, it was there that my daughter, Gaillimh, one of the greatest treasures of my life, was drowned in the river which runs into the sea. Her mother before her had also drowned while Gaillimh was still only a baby and I was left to raise her alone. Her brothers Brian and Oscar (looking to indicate his two young companions) were almost young men at the time. After their mother was lost to the sea, Gaillimh became my constant source of love and happiness. I could have lived out my life quite content, but when the sea also took her, I lost all reason. Even my bravest and swiftest warriors could not save her. We put to sea and searched for a long time, but no trace of her was ever found.'

He paused for a moment and everyone remained silent.

'Because of this tragedy, I could find no comfort but only sorrow in my life. So one day, shortly afterwards, I set out to sea with my two sons. I cursed Manannán Mac Lir for not protecting Gaillimh and her mother. After all, he was guardian of the sea and I believed that he could have saved them. Manannán was very angry. He said that no human could disrespect him in such a manner, but in my anguish I cursed him repeatedly. He became so angry that he banished me from Ireland and sent me to the Land of the Lonely, a part of Tír na nÓg where I would find only eternal loneliness.'

The following day, Brasil gathered his people together on the stony foreshore of the bay at Galway and told them that he and his sons were leaving to live on an island far to the west. 'We have remained here since that time – some now call this island Hy-Brasil and believe that it takes its name from me, but Tír na nÓg is much older than I, and existed long, long before my time.'

Feeling sorry for him, Danielle asked if he had ever returned to see his home.

'From time to time, Manannán Mac Lir allows me to ride across the ocean so I can gaze upon my former kingdom, but it is no longer the place that I remember or could call home. Time has moved on since I ruled from my great fort at Dangan. It has suffered the ravages of time and today it is completely overgrown with trees and wild vegetation. Many people do not even know of its existence, let alone its importance in ancient times.'

While he was speaking, David was thinking how he had once visited that old fort, but he was not in the form for talking, so he did not mention it. Although lonely themselves, Niamh and the children felt great sorrow for Brasil.

Brasil said that he remembered seeing the children upon their arrival in Tír na nÓg. Niamh explained to him how she had brought the children here and of their fate since they arrived.

'Your father has already explained much of what you have told me, Niamh,' he said.

Before Brasil could say another word, she interrupted him, and asked if there was any possibility of returning the children to their own time and place.

Looking at the children, he replied, 'I know how your parents are feeling right now, but I do not know if there is a way to return you to your own time.'

He was silent for a moment and then added, 'But perhaps Manannán Mac Lir holds the answer to your question. He is almost as old as time itself, and as guardian of the sea possesses great knowledge. I will ride out to sea myself and try to find him. I need to talk with him privately.'

The king knew that Brasil was serious about making this journey alone, and smiling said, 'Be careful my friend – that old sea guardian may still be angry with you.'

'Perhaps, but I hope the years have mellowed him.'

Brasil then turned to his sons. 'You shall accompany me only as far as the seashore. The rest of you can await my return at the castle.'

The three of them then rode off into the distance and on reaching the sea Brasil continued alone.

Manannán Mac Lir

Once he reached the open ocean Brasil began calling out for Manannán Mac Lir. After a short time, a mermaid surfaced and asked him why he was looking for her king.

He told her who he was and said that it was very important that he spoke with Manannán Mac Lir.

'I will go to his palace and let him know that you are awaiting him,' she said.

The mermaid then leaped into the air and dived almost straight down into the sea. Her long tail was the last he saw of her as she slipped beneath the waves without disturbing the calmness of the ocean.

After some time, a great wave rose up before him. It continued to build until it was about ten metres high, but remained suspended, not advancing or subsiding, just holding its position. As he watched, a large tunnel of swirling water appeared in the wave and he heard a voice calling to him from inside the great wall of water.

He cautiously moved his horse forward until he was closer to the entrance, then suddenly, Manannán Mac Lir, mounted on a great golden chariot pulled by four enormous sea horses, burst through the opening in the wave and halted before him. His long red hair and beard were a mass of curls, and his green robes were open at the chest.

'Why have you summoned me?' he asked in a strong deep voice.

'I seek your wisdom. Not for myself,' said Brasil, 'but for others, who have been unfortunate.'

Brasil told him what had happened to the children and the loss that their families must have felt and finished by saying, 'I know only too well the sorrow of losing family to the sea.'

'Why have you come to me?' Manannán Mac Lir asked. 'I am not responsible for what has happened to these children!'

'I am aware of this,' replied Brasil, 'but I have come to ask you if there is any way of turning back time?'

'No, but there is a way that one can return through time and change an event before it occurs,' the great sea guardian said, 'but I cannot help you. There is only one who guards the doors and passage of time and he is not of this kingdom.'

'Who is this person?' asked Brasil.

'He is not a person, he is Janus – the guardian of the past, present and future. The one who guards the entrances and exits to other worlds. He is a guardian with two faces – one which looks deep into the past, the other that looks forward into the future,' said Manannán.

He then told Brasil how to make contact with Janus. 'But first you must find the Janus Stone. It is a carved-stone image of his head which also has two faces. But I have no idea of its location for no one has sought its power for centuries.'

Before leaving, Brasil asked about his wife and daughter.

'If you seek the Janus Stone because you wish to return through time to prevent their deaths, then you must take great care as some-one will have to take their place and forfeit their own lives. Brasil, you must understand that I am not responsible for the death of your family. I look after the sea kingdom, and have no power over life or death – there is a much greater force in the universe that determines when it is time for someone to die, and none of us can question that wisdom. I can only tell you that your family awaits the day when it is your time to join them.'

Brasil hesitated for a moment and then said, 'I have spent many lonely and bitter years blaming you for my misfortune and thinking only of myself. It is time for me to change all of this.'

He thanked Manannán Mac Lir for his advice and turned his horse to begin his journey back to Tír na nÓg.

Arriving at the castle, Brasil went inside and was greeted by one of the servants, who took him to the room where his two sons, Queen Edain, Niamh and the children were seated around a banquet table. From the head of the table, the king called on Brasil to sit and join them.

Before he was even seated, Niamh asked if there was a way to return the children to their own time.

Brasil told them of his meeting with Manannán Mac Lir, and explained how Janus was the only one with the power to help.

'How can we find him?' Luke asked.

Brasil said that Manannán Mac Lir told him that they must first seek the Janus Stone; a stone image with two faces, one young and the other old. 'Once it is found, it must then be taken to Tara, the ancient seat of the Irish high kings, and placed upon the Stone of Destiny. When the dawn sun penetrates the young face of the stone, it will carry on through to the old. The sunlight will create a channel of light and when it strikes the earth Janus will know he is being summoned. Only he can open a gateway to the past, but if he agrees to help us, he will issue certain warnings that must be heeded.'

'So this means that we can travel back through time,' the king said.

'Yes,' replied Brasil.

Niamh – unable to contain her emotion – interrupted them , saying, 'Then we will be able to take the children home?'

'Perhaps,' Brasil replied. 'But first we must find the Janus Stone and even then it is a dangerous journey to travel back through time.'

Excited at these developments and thinking aloud, Niamh asked if it would be possible for her to return to ancient Ireland after they brought the children home.

'You wish to find Oisín?' he said.

Remembering what Manannán Mac Lir had said, Brasil warned, 'If you are thinking about trying to save him, an exchange of lives will have to be made. But there is no need to discuss such matters right now. We must first find the Janus Stone – it is only then we can make contact with Janus.'

The Janus Stone

David listened closely to all Brasil had to say and just as Niamh was about to ask another question, he blurted out, 'I have seen the stone head.'

Everyone fell silent as his words echoed around the banquet hall.

They were all surprised at David's sudden disclosure. He then told them about how he had fallen into the underground cavern as he was chasing a fox, of being frightened by the phantoms and of his meeting with Cian, who had set him free.

'You will take us to this underground place,' said Niamh.

'Of course,' David said. 'But the entrance is dangerous and deep.'

'That will not be a problem,' King Aengus said immediately. 'We will prepare at once.'

David then explained how Cian had told him that if the Janus Stone was removed it would have serious consequences, but he did not know what they would be.

'We will have to do something,' Niamh said, looking around the table. 'We will go to Cian and seek his advice. There must be something that he can do.'

Luke was now feeling bothered about what he had said to David earlier, and said, 'Sorry, David.'

'It's OK, Luke. I should have told you earlier.' He had not spoken since the argument in the Land of the Lonely.

There was a glimmer of hope and everyone was talking together. They were all questioning how such a place could exist in Tír na nÓg without anyone knowing of it.

The king then called out in a loud voice, 'Silence please.'

Looking at his wife, he said, 'I know that your father instructed me never to divulge the secrets of Tír na nÓg when I was crowned king all those centuries ago. However, because of all that has happened, the time has now come when I must reveal at least one of them. I am sure, Edain, that he would come to the same decision if he were here right now.'

'I am also sure, Aengus, that he would do all in his power to help the children,' the queen said, 'so I agree that the time has come to disclose this secret.'

The king then told all those present about the existence of this place in his kingdom, and that it was a royal secret.

'It is the secret place of the ancients and knowledge of its existence is only passed down from the kings and queens of this land to their successors. A vow of secrecy must be taken when there is a change in rulers. Its existence was never to be revealed to anyone, no matter who they were. Great danger could befall Tír na nÓg if the privacy of this secret place was not respected.'

He told them that the forest is said to have been haunted since ancient times and that this story was encouraged by every king of Tír na nÓg.

'That is why people are warned not to stray from the forest path. I feel that there will be changes in Tír na nÓg, otherwise how could David have just stumbled on an entrance to the underworld? I don't believe that things happen by accident or coincidence!'

'I was only chasing a fox,' David said. 'I told you that already.'

'What fox? Did anyone else see a fox?' asked the king.

There was no reply.

'David will take us to where he fell into the chamber,' the king said, and then ordered his men to saddle the horses.

Before leaving, King Aengus swore all those present to secrecy.

Once they reached the forest, the king said, 'David, you will have to lead us from here, as only you know the location of the entrance.'

When they reached the place where David had seen the fox, they all dismounted and followed him into the overgrown forest. They searched and searched the area until they located the hole in the earth where David had fallen. King Aengus ordered Gearóid to tie a rope around the trunk of a nearby tree and then, grabbing the rope, he lowered himself into the ground. When he reached the bottom of the shaft he stood for a few moments until his eyes grew accustomed to the darkness. He saw the green light – the light that David had told them about – looming out from the chamber at the end of the passage. One by one, the others climbed down into the passage and once they were all together, the king led the way into the chamber.

'I will do exactly as I did before,' David said as he made his way towards the Stone of Envy. Having removed the stone, the phantoms soon began to appear, calling for the return of the stone. Danielle and Luke became frightened and stood close to Niamh, grabbing on to her cloak as the phantoms became louder and more menacing. David walked towards the huge stone from which Cian had emerged earlier.

After a few moments, the figure of the ancient warrior began to emerge from the stone. They all stood still and looked on in amazement as they heard David apologise to Cian.

'Are we to have our world constantly invaded by mortals?' asked Cian.

David explained why he had returned with the others, who were now gathered before Cian.

Danielle then approached Cian and said, 'I'm sorry, but all we want to do is go home.'

'I cannot help you,' Cian replied.

Brasil, who was behind the others, said, 'Yes you can, Cian,' his voice being almost drowned out by the sound of the phantoms.

'Silence,' Cian shouted, giving even Niamh and the children a fright; and the chamber went quiet immediately.

'It is you, Brasil,' said Cian, looking beyond the others. 'Your people and mine were once sworn enemies, but I must honour you as a great and noble warrior of our ancient past. Why have you come to me for help, Brasil – what can I do? As you see, we are now part of the underworld and cannot even venture into the beautiful kingdom that exists above.'

Cian listened as Brasil told him of the children's plight, of his meeting with Manannán Mac Lir, how they required the stone image of Janus to perform the time ritual at Tara and open a gateway to the past.

Cian was silent for some moments, and then said, 'It is very important that you all listen carefully to what I am going to tell you. I have already given David one reason why the stone head is located in this sacred place, but I did not give him the second and most important reason as he did not need to know this at the time. This is a very dangerous request that you have placed upon me. There was a purpose in having the Janus Stone located in this place.'

Cian then explained that it was through the magic of the stone that the Formorians, an ancient and evil race of giants, were suspended in time and unable to enter any dominion. They had caused great sorrow throughout the ancient world. 'However,' he said, 'many centuries ago they were trapped in a spirit realm by Janus, the keeper of the gateway to other worlds. The only way that they can escape is through the underworld of Tír na nÓg, as it is the only place that has survived intact since those ancient times.' He told them that the stone head was placed in the chamber by Janus himself, who assured him that while it was located there the Formorians could never escape. The stone must always remain under the protection of the Dé Danaan spirits and must not be removed by anyone. He also warned Cian that if the stone was ever removed and not returned before sunset on the third day, then Tír na nÓg as they knew it would cease to exist.

Niamh was shocked and asked, 'How could this happen?'

'Once the stone is removed, the Druids of the Formorians will know. Remember, the most evil of all the Formorians is the one-eyed Balor, whose gaze turns his enemies to stone. My son Lugh defeated him in combat, but he still exists in the spirit world, just awaiting his chance to return. Janus allowed the Formorians to accompany him to the spirit world, but once they had all passed through, he closed the gateway, trapping them there. Once Balor senses the possibility of escape, he will gather his forces and ask his Druids to open the gateway into this world, which will take three days. If the Formorians do escape they will seek out the most powerful weapon of the ancient world, the Key to Time and with this they can enter any realm they wish and bring great terror and destruction with them. So now you understand the absolute importance of keeping the Janus Stone in this sacred place.

'Janus placed a great trust and responsibility upon me, and now I must place the same trust and responsibility upon you. You need to understand that when I release the stone of Janus it must be returned within three days or the sacred power of this chamber will diminish and the Formorians will gain access to Tír na nÓg and destroy centuries of happiness in just days. Remember that Balor was also a sorcerer and if he regains his mortal status he will seek out the ancient Stone of Balor, from which he draws his power. It is vital you return the Janus Stone within the time constraints set before you.'

Brasil remembered the terror the Formorians had once brought

to Ireland and agreed with Cian, telling all present that if this was to happen then not only would Tír na nÓg be in danger, but Ireland also.

'Remember,' Cian said, 'you only need the head to summon Janus. Once he appears, the head has completed its task and the key, which he retains, is all that is needed to open the passage of time.'

Once everyone knew the importance and danger of the mission on which they were about to embark, Brasil said, 'No time can be lost,' and called on his sons to remove the Janus Stone. He turned to Cian and assured him that, one way or another, they would return within three days and restore the head.

As it was being removed, David noticed the ancient face carved on the opposite side of the stone. He thanked Cian for all his help and returned the glowing green Stone of Envy to the now empty hollow. He turned and said goodbye to Cian, and then ran towards the passage to join the others. When they were back on the pathway in the forest, it was agreed that only Brasil, his sons, Niamh and the children would go to Tara.

They all went back to the castle where the king and queen wished the children a successful journey. They had grown very fond of them over the past few days and reminded them that no matter what happened they would always have a home in Tír na nÓg.

When they had mounted their horses in front of the castle, King Aengus said, 'It will be nightfall before you reach Ireland; this is good as you can cross the country under cover of darkness because you will not remain invisible on land, only on the sea. Your horses are swift, so you should reach Tara before sunrise.'

Gearóid and some of the warriors escorted them as far as the ocean. During the journey, Niamh noticed that Gearóid was not at all friendly towards her and was a little troubled by his behaviour. However, she was so concerned about what lay ahead of them that she decided that she would not question him until her return.

To Tara and Janus

They galloped over the ocean towards Ireland and when they reached the western shore they continued at speed across the country. They arrived at the Hill of Tara just before dawn the following morning. Niamh reminded all of them not to dismount under any circumstances and to be careful not to fall from their horses.

Brasil ordered his sons to remove the head from the sack and place it on the Stone of Destiny, so that the young face was turned towards the rising sun. They all waited and watched intently as the sun began to appear on the eastern horizon. While they waited, Brasil's thoughts returned to ancient Ireland and Tara, and the great banquets held in its once magnificent royal halls. He thought of the great feats of courage displayed by the warriors of those times. However, he was saddened as he looked out over the ever-brightening landscape of modern Ireland, with its huge modern roads, houses and the ruins of 'his' ancient world. He no longer recognised the land which he had once helped rule. Niamh and his sons were also astonished to see all the changes.

Finally, the sun cleared the horizon and shone directly onto the youthful face of the stone image. As the sunlight penetrated the stone through its open mouths, the effect was dramatic on the opposite side. There was a circle of darkness located at the end of a long, dark shadow extending across the ground caused by the stone head mounted on the Stone of Destiny. The shaft of light that penetrated the head was surrounded by the dark circle as it struck the earth, some twenty metres away.

As they gazed at the light, it became larger and more intense, turning almost pure white, but it was not blinding. There was a tremendous rumbling in the ground and the light seemed to be sucked into a hole in the earth. The tunnel grew larger and larger, and a few moments later a horseman emerged from the tunnel of light and halted in front of the group. There was momentary silence, and then the rider asked why they had summoned his presence.

It was Janus. His youthful face resembled that of the stone image, as did his shoulder-length black hair. He wore clothes that looked similar to that of an ancient Celtic warrior and carried a large, highly decorated, golden staff with an ornate circular loop in his right hand.

When he had settled his horse, he looked at the stone head and asked why it had been removed from the chamber. He sounded a little angry, but Brasil and Niamh explained the situation regarding the children. He then asked if Cian had explained the danger of removing the Janus Stone. They assured him that he had, and that they would ensure that it was returned as soon as the ceremony was complete. Indicating to his sons, Brasil said, 'This is the reason for my sons accompanying me to Tara.'

Janus seemed satisfied.

Niamh asked him if she could return to find Oisín having returned the children to their own time. Janus told her that it was possible, but warned her that if she wished to save Oisín from his fate, then someone would have to take his place as he had already suffered death.

Niamh thought about this for a few moments and said, 'I just wish to return to see him and say goodbye forever; perhaps then I will find inner peace.'

Turning his older face towards them, Janus said that his youthful face took him forward through time and his older face back through time. All were astonished by the image before them; his face was now ancient-looking, and he had shoulder-length grey hair and beard.

'I know exactly when and where you must exit the tunnel; the children will return home first, then you can continue to find Oisín; he will be searching for his father and his friends when you arrive, so you must wait for him close to the sea.'

He told them that the gateway through the Tunnel of Ages was now open, but warned that it was a dangerous journey to undertake. 'I cannot accompany you because I am the only one who can protect the entrance, which must be kept open until you have reached your first destination. Once I enter the Tunnel of Ages, it will close so rapidly behind me that only my horse is swift enough to keep ahead of it.'

He also warned them that once they entered the tunnel, their horses would gallop at an incredible speed, and if for any reason they fell, they would exit into another dimension and time. 'If this happens, even I may not be able to rescue you.' He explained that they could enter a dimension during a time of war or famine and perish before he would be able to locate them.

Janus also told them that the journey would be very frightening as they would be passing back through time and would catch fleeting glimpses of phantoms, ghost-like images, and the decay of centuries. Holding out the golden staff in his right hand, Janus said, 'I will give you the Key to Time and when you hold it aloft its power will penetrate the correct exit in the Tunnel of Ages at the given time.'

'How will we know where to exit?' Danielle asked.

'You will hear my voice calling out 'Your time is close', and five seconds later my facial image will materialise before you. It will be large and have a ghost-like appearance. Do not stop, as the image will continue to move ahead of you; just slow the horses down. Be warned, you have only ten seconds to make the exit; whoever holds the key must ride in front and call out "OPEN IN THE NAME OF JANUS" when the image appears. It will become very bright, growing bigger and bigger, until it forms into a large bright circle – the same as the one you are now about to enter. It will then slow down, allowing you to reach it at the appointed time. This is your exit, and once you pass through it, only then can I enter the Tunnel of Ages and follow you to retrieve the key.'

They all thanked Janus, and Brasil told his sons that, no matter what happened, they must return the head to Tír na nÓg once Janus had entered the tunnel. He thanked them both for centuries of loyalty, and leaned out of the saddle to hug each of them in turn, and told them that he loved them. They looked at him somewhat curiously, and Brian said, 'You will be returning father.'

'My sons, my fate is in the hands of God. Once you have reached Tír na nÓg you will know if we have been successful. Niamh should be there to greet you both.'

Brasil reached out and took the key from Janus and, turning to Niamh, said, 'I will ride ahead, with the children just behind me, and you will ride at the rear.'

She nodded in agreement and they moved their horses into position – as they were now ready for the journey back through time.

Turning to his sons again, Brasil said, 'Brian, Oscar, you know what you have to do. The Janus Stone must be returned to Cian's chamber with great speed. You must not stop until you have completed this task.'

They told him to have no fear, that they would complete their mission, and then wished them all a safe journey.

The horses were growing impatient and excited, and just before they moved off, Brasil told the children that no matter what happened they should remain behind him at all times. They all faced the Tunnel of Ages and the intense light coming from the opening. Brasil called out, 'First to Inishmaan with the children and then on to find Oisín', as they rode forward in the agreed formation.

Danielle, David and Luke were excited but frightened at the same time. Before they fully realised it, they were riding through the gateway of time.

Strange sensations shot through their young bodies as they passed through the gateway. The sudden jolt of the horses as they took off into a full gallop shocked them into the reality of the danger they now faced.

Tunnel of Ages

Once inside the tunnel, it grew a little darker, but they could all still see each other. The horses continued to gather momentum until, as Janus had told them, they were travelling at unnatural speeds. As they galloped through the tunnel, phantom figures began to appear and disappear on each side of the riders. Shouts of joy, anger and suffering could also be heard continuously as they rode back through the centuries.

Luke was directly behind Brasil and was becoming more and more concerned about the phantoms now looming from almost every part of the tunnel; even the horses seemed spooked. Their nostrils were snorting heavily and sweat drenched their fine coats. The sound of their hooves echoed and seemed almost ghostly as they galloped along. Hundreds of skull-like ghostly images occupied almost every section of the tunnel, and decrepit, withered arms seemed to be reaching out as if trying to grab at them. All the while shrieks and moans echoed throughout the journey.

Danielle closed her eyes as she held tightly onto the horse's mane as well as the reins. David seemed to be managing best of the children, and although frightened of the speed at which the horses were now travelling, he was excited by the experience. Such was the swiftness of the animals, Niamh's long flowing hair stretched back almost the length of her horse. Her heart was filled with hope that she could bring the children home and, of course, meet Oisín. It made the frightening journey worthwhile.

After a time, they heard Janus call out, 'Your time is close!' and,

sure enough, his image appeared before them five seconds later. Brasil began to raise the Key to Time in one hand and, as he did so, pulled on the reins with the other to slow his horse. He called out to the children, telling them this was where they were about to leave the tunnel.

Luke, who was terrified at this stage, did not heed his orders fast enough and his horse collided into the back of Brasil's, causing him to lose his balance. In an effort to regain control, Brasil immediately grabbed the reins of the horse with both hands, but in doing so the key slipped from his grasp and shot up into the air. He called out in panic, 'I've lost the key!'

The speed of the horses was such, that the key had not fallen to the bottom of the tunnel before David's horse passed it. As fast as lightning, David, who had seen what had happened and heard Brasil shout, reached out and grabbed the key as it flew past him while shouting out at the top of his voice to Brasil, who was looking around in horror at the thought of having lost the key, 'It's OK.

I've caught it!' David's days of playing hurling had finally paid off.

Although it all happened in seconds, it was too late. The image of Janus had disappeared and they had missed the exit; ridden right through and continued along the Tunnel of Ages. Brasil called out, 'We missed the exit but we cannot stop. We must continue back to Oisín's time and decide on what to do.'

He then called for David to catch up quickly and pass him the key. Phantoms and screams surrounded them and a now very frightened David rode his horse even harder as Brasil and Luke tried to slow their horses down a little. Panic was setting in with all of them, and the thought of missing their exit worried the children and added to the terror of the tunnel.

However, David did not have too much time to dwell on this thought as he was so intent on his responsibility in returning the key to Brasil. It took some time, but he managed to pass Luke and eventually came level with Brasil.

Just at that moment, they heard the call again from Janus –

'Your time is close!' and again the image appeared before them.

David attempted to reach out and pass the key over to Brasil, who shouted, 'No, no, it's too late, you must give the command yourself. NOW, NOW!' he shouted.

In panic, David, now riding side by side with Brasil, raised the key and called out, 'OPEN IN THE NAME OF JANUS!'

An extremely strong ray of light shone directly from the loop of the key and onto the face of the image. It immediately started to change form and began swirling around and around, growing larger and larger. The darkened tunnel ahead of them disappeared and soon they were riding out through a large bright opening into a lush green landscape. Once they had all cleared the exit, they settled the horses down and gave them a few minutes' rest.

They were breathless themselves, but exhilarated. At first, every-one was silent trying to come to terms with what had just happened. After a few minutes Brasil said, 'You did well, David.'

He just nodded in agreement, as he was shaking with fright.

'Well done, David,' Danielle also said, reaching over, pulling him towards her and planting a kiss on his cheek. David's face turned bright red and his head dropped with embarrassment. The others laughed a little, but they all agreed that he had done very well. Danielle was about to say something to Luke about them missing their exit, but held back; David did not, and told him he should not be let ride an ass, let alone a horse. Luke was about to reply using some strong language, but Brasil intervened, telling the boys that they could sort this out later; there were more pressing matters to attend to right now.

'We have to get you back to your own time, but first we must find Oisín,' he said.

Niamh's heart leapt at the thought of meeting her long-lost love after the centuries of loneliness.

Reunion of Oisín and Niamh

B rasil lead the way towards the sea, which was some distance away, and soon they were all riding across high ground overlooking the ocean. A welcome sea breeze hit their faces as they brought their horses to a halt. Looking inland as far as the eye could see, there were no roads, no houses, no fences, not even a stone wall, in fact nothing man-made could be seen – just a beautiful green landscape dotted here and there with huge trees. Even the air had a strange freshness about it. When Danielle commented on this, Brasil said, 'There is no decay here – the air and water is completely clean and free of any poisons.'

'Where are we?' Luke asked.

'Ireland – ancient Ireland,' replied Brasil.

'How long before Oisín will arrive?' asked Danielle.

'I don't know,' Niamh said, 'but we must look out for men moving large stones if Gavin's story is correct about Oisín helping them and falling off his horse.'

As they continued along the headland, Niamh was becoming a little anxious; Brasil tried to reassure her that Oisín must be close. As they rode along, they were all watching the shoreline, except for Luke. Movement on a hillside some distance away attracted him. Suddenly, it dawned on him that the movement was workmen building a circular stone structure – a large stone ringfort – similar to the one at home on Inishmaan.

'Look,' he shouted, pointing to the hillside, 'there are men over there moving large rocks.'

The group halted and Brasil said, 'We will go and ask if they have seen any strangers.' As they approached, they noticed a rider coming from another direction. He was closer to the men on the hillside. Suddenly, Niamh forced her horse out in front of the others and galloped away at high speed over the rolling landscape towards the lone rider.

She was screaming, 'NO, NO, NO ...' at the top of her voice. The others followed her, gathering speed as they went.

The men on the hillside heard her shouts first and were very confused. They also saw the strange rider who was almost upon them. As he halted, he heard Niamh call out again and turned his horse to face her as she galloped towards him. As she reached him, a voice she had not heard for centuries called out to her, 'Niamh, what are you doing here? Why have you followed me?'

As she reached him, Niamh leaned over and kissed and hugged Oisín with one arm, saying, 'Oh Oisín, I have missed you so much – the centuries without you have been terrible.'

She had not planned to tell him this immediately, but was so overcome with emotion that she could not contain herself.

Oisín was confused. He had no idea what she was talking about. 'But I only left two days ago, Niamh. I was just on my way home to you,' he replied.

Niamh was trying to explain all that had happened since he left Tír na nÓg, when the others reached the hillside. He was now even more confused as he looked at Brasil and the children.

The children were astonished. Here before them, mounted on a huge chestnut-coloured horse, was Oisín, the great warrior poet of the Fianna. Hundreds of thousands of people over the centuries had heard the stories of this man, but most did not believe that he had even existed.

It really is Oisín, David thought. His features were strong and noble with long fair hair swept back from his face and secured with a red band around his forehead. His beard was red and golden, and his eyes were a piercing blue-green, like the ocean. His long blue cloak hung down each side of his body and was embroidered with various Celtic designs in gold, silver and bronze. Underneath was a white tunic, and he wore a chain around his neck, from which hung a medallion. His trousers were brown and tied criss-crossed from the knees down with whitish leather straps. His shoes were made from soft hide, and a highly decorated sword hung from his brown leather belt. His silver oval shield hung from one side of his horse, polished so brightly that it reflected the sunlight like a mirror.

As the children looked on in amazement, Niamh and Brasil explained the situation as best they could. Even the men who were working on the fort stopped what they were doing and looked on in bewilderment at Oisín and Niamh, as well as at the children, who also looked foreign to them.

The children heard Oisín say, 'So I am going to die today. This cannot be changed.'

Tears welled up in Niamh's eyes as she said, 'Yes Oisín, but I will dismount with you. I cannot face an eternity in Tír na nÓg without you.'

She turned towards Brasil and said, 'Brasil will see that the children get home safely.'

'No,' Brasil said, 'I will take Oisín's place this day.'

Niamh was shocked, and after a few moments began to protest.

'You are willing to die in my place, Brasil?' Oisín asked.

'Not really die in your place,' came the reply, 'but to join my wife and daughter, whom I lost centuries ago. I am an old man now and have spent many centuries a sad and lonely man in the most beautiful kingdom on earth.'

They were about to interrupt him, but Brasil raised his hand and said, 'Silence. Please, listen to me. Tell my sons that I truly love them, but this is something I must do. It is a journey on which I must venture alone. Tell them they have both served me loyally and it is time for them to move away from the Land of the Lonely and find the happiness they so richly deserve in the Land of Eternal Youth. I am sure that they will understand my decision in time. I go now, satisfied in the knowledge that I will bring some degree of happiness to my sons by releasing them from my service, and indeed, to you, Niamh. You know the pain of losing someone you love, and you have suffered centuries of loneliness in your father's beautiful kingdom. But you were never bitter; you were always kind and caring to everyone. Your smile and kindness will always remain a part of the beauty of Tír na nÓg. Your love for Oisín has spanned centuries and it is time you reaped the just rewards of your perseverance. You and Oisín are still young and deserve a second chance at happiness together. I have given this matter much thought over the past few days and I know it is the right decision. For centuries I have been known as a lonely and bitter old man, but at least now I will be remembered for having given some measure of happiness to people.'

They all knew that Brasil had made up his mind and that he would not change his decision. Oisín tried to protest, but Brasil would not budge. He then urged his horse forward towards Brasil and reached out to shake his hand.

Niamh moved closer, on the opposite side to Oisín, and hugged Brasil as tears ran down her cheeks. They both thanked him for the sacrifice he was about to make and told him that he would never be forgotten.

'I will explain to Brian and Oscar. I am sure that they have been honoured and proud to serve one of the greatest Irish chieftains,' Oisín said.

The children pressed forward also and reached out and shook Brasil's hand, telling him that although they were frightened of never reaching home again, they were privileged to have met him and would never forget him.

David then told him how he had once visited his old fort at Dangan and would do so again and take his friends there. He would tell them it was once the fort of a great Irish chieftain.

Brasil smiled and said, 'Thank you, David, and remember that it is still a place of wonder.'

Then looking at the others, he said, 'Now it's time you all went home.'

Just then, some of the men who were involved in building the fort approached and asked for help in moving the large stones into place in the final section of the structure. Brasil smiled at the little group gathered around him and said, 'My time is now.'

'I just wish to ask these people one question,' Oisín said.

Brasil nodded as Oisín asked the men did they know, or had they ever heard of, the great Celtic chieftain Fionn Mac Cumhail and the Fianna.

'Of course,' one of the men replied, and all the others nodded in agreement. He told Oisín that the Fianna had died many hundreds of years ago.

One of them then said that Fionn Mac Cumhail had a son, Oisín, a warrior poet, but that he had disappeared hundreds of years ago and no one knew what had happened to him. He had been enchanted away by a beautiful princess from some distant land across the sea and never returned to his homeland.

Oisín was saddened; he knew now for sure that his old world was gone forever.

Niamh sensed his loneliness for the old ways, and reached out to him, saying, 'They will never be forgotten. Oisín. Down through the centuries Fionn and the Fianna will provide entertainment and fascination to countless generations of children and adults alike. Their memory will never die; stories of the Fianna will be told, retold and embellished through time. They will always be remembered.'

Brasil then said to the men, 'You can go back to your work. I will join you shortly, but first I must say goodbye to my friends.'

He wished Niamh and Oisín great happiness together, and told the children that this had been a great adventure for him and thanked them for bringing back to life feelings that he thought had long since vanished from his soul. 'You must go now. I will not dismount until you have entered the Tunnel of Ages.'

He turned his horse towards the workmen at the fort and rode up to join them.

Return Home

Niamh, Oisín and the children were reluctant to leave; they sat on their horses watching Brasil until he reached the workmen. Looking back, Brasil called out to them, 'You must leave now.'

'There must be another way – I cannot allow this to happen,' Oisín said.

'There is no other way; you are not responsible for what has happened, Oisín. It was I who insisted on finding you,' Niamh said.

Just as Oisín was about to reply, Brasil shouted again in a louder voice, 'You must leave right now. Take the children home, Niamh, and don't forget to tell my sons that this was the only way home for me.'

Oisín turned and, looking at Niamh, said, 'I cannot let him do this.'

'Please, please, Oisín – think of what Brasil has said. He has spent centuries in the Land of the Lonely and does not wish to return to that life. You were not there, Oisín; you have no idea of what it was like for him. I am not being selfish – I would gladly forfeit my life to be with you, but Brasil has made his decision and nothing will change it. The thought of returning to Tír na nÓg alone is too painful for him, as it is for me.'

Oisín knew that Niamh was right.

Niamh then called out to Brasil, 'I will never be able to repay you, Brasil, but I will never forget you.'

'My thanks is in your beautiful smile, Niamh, and in the know-

ledge that I have given you much happiness,' Brasil shouted. 'Please go now; it is time to take the children home.'

They all waved one last time, then turned their horses and rode back to where they had made their entrance into this ancient world. They could see from a distance that there was a horseman waiting where the exit from the Tunnel of Ages had been. It was Janus. When they reached him, his youthful face awaited them.

Janus asked Niamh why the children had missed their exit, and she explained what had happened. He then informed them that Brian and Oscar were already on the way back to Tír na nÓg with the Janus Stone, and, looking at Oisín, he noticed that Brasil was missing.

Meanwhile, back at the fort, Brasil addressed the workmen, saying, 'I will help you, but first you must send for your holy preacher, Patrick. I have much to tell him.'

A short time later 'Saint Patrick', the preacher of the new faith, came down to hear what Brasil had to say. He listened intently to the stories of Tír na nÓg and Oisín and Niamh, writing it all down as Brasil spoke. When he finished, he told the workmen, whom he had agreed to help, that he would have to work fast as there would be little time left for him once his feet touched the ground.

Brasil then dismounted and, before his powerful strength failed him, moved the huge boulders into place in the fort. He then sat on the ground and, already growing weak, began to change dramatically as the centuries spent in Tír na nÓg caught up on him. As he grew weaker, all his features began to change; his body became extremely thin and frail. The workmen stood in shock – even Patrick; they were all staring in disbelief at the ancient figure now collapsed on the ground before them. Looking up at them, Brasil said in a weakened voice, 'Remember all I have told you, Patrick – do not let the legend of Tír na nÓg die with me.'

Niamh explained to Janus about Brasil's decision to take Oisín's place.

After Oisín thanked Janus for all his help, he asked that he take the children back to Tír na nÓg and from there take them home.

Janus became a little alarmed and said to him, 'No, you must return with the children to their time and place on Inishmaan first. Then both of you can return to Tír na nÓg together from Inishmaan – you cannot return from here.'

They all looked at Janus a little confused.

'Niamh, it was during your search for Oisín that you encountered the children. If you return to Tír na nÓg directly from here, then your quest to find Oisín will never have happened. It is many centuries before the birth of the children. From Inishmaan, both of you can finally return to Tír na nÓg together and you will be there in time to greet Brian and Oscar when they arrive, and give them the news of their father. It is time to go now. Who will carry the Key to Time?'

'David,' Niamh said, 'you brought us here, you take us home.'

David felt his heart pounding in his chest but knew that he must be strong. 'Hold on to your horse, Luke,' he said as he smiled at Danielle. Raising the key high above his head, he shouted, 'OPEN IN THE NAME OF JANUS '. A flash of light shone from the loop of the key and opened a large bright swirling tunnel before them. Soon, they were all charging into the tunnel and forward through the centuries.

After what seemed like ages riding, Luke, again uneasy, called out, 'Are we there yet?'

David was about to answer him when he heard the command, 'Your time is close!' and, like a professional horseman at this stage, raised the key in one hand while controlling the animal with the other, and called out the magic words, 'OPEN IN THE NAME OF JANUS', as soon as the image appeared.

The large bright opening appeared before them and soon they were riding out onto the beach at Inishmaan. They brought their horses to a halt and again rested them, while looking around. Although their surroundings were very familiar, the children were wondering if they had returned at the right moment in time. It seemed like they were gone for ages because so much had happened since they left home on that sunny morning. Had they returned to the correct time and how would they know?

Just then, there was a shout from the headland. It was Danielle's sister Chloe, calling for her to come home for her lunch. Chloe was very confused to see all of them on horseback, and two adults dressed in the strangest clothes with them.

'I think it is safe to dismount now,' Niamh said.

'I think Luke should dismount first as he caused most of our problems,' said David, smiling.

A very reluctant Luke began to ease his way carefully off the horse. He soon stood on the ground with his eyes tightly closed, and asked, 'Am I changing?'

'It's too late now if you are – your horse has already started its journey out to sea,' David said, and they all began to laugh.

David and Danielle dismounted together, and their horses also turned and made their way out to sea. Niamh looked down at her three young friends, saddened that she would never see them again. She thought about the amazing adventures they'd had, and how the journey not only restored the children to their own time, but also reunited her with her long-lost love. She told them that she would never forget them and that they were now part of the legend of Tír na nÓg.

She said that they had brought great happiness to Tír na nÓg; but for them, Brasil and his sons would still be in the Land of the Lonely, trapped in centuries of solitude. Looking at Oisín, she reached out, took his hand and said, 'My great warrior poet would be dead and I would be condemned to a life of unending loneliness in the Land of Eternal Youth.'

Oisín also thanked the children and told them to remember that when they walked along the headland of the island, to look out over the ocean and, if the day was clear, to keep a good eye on the horizon, and maybe, just maybe, they would be lucky enough to catch another glimpse of Tír na nÓg.

'Remember,' Niamh said, 'this happens every seven years so some day you may see our island again. Just remember today's date, and remember us. Today is 24 May 2004, the day that Tír na nÓg revealed some of its magic, and it is also our very special day – the day when Oisín and I were reunited after centuries.'

Having said goodbye, Niamh and Oisín turned their horses and, waving to the children, were soon galloping away across the ocean. The children watched Oisín and Niamh fade and disappear as the magic of Tír na nÓg began to conceal them. The three of them stood in silence for some time, not fully believing all that had happened to them in just one morning. No one would believe them, so Tír na nÓg would remain a mystery and the children's most wonderful secret.

Suddenly, another shout from the headland broke the spell. It was Chloe again, calling to Danielle to tell her that she was to come home right away – that their mother was wondering where she had been all morning. The three of them ran towards her, almost unable to contain their excitement.

Upon reaching the headland, Chloe said to Luke, 'You're for it when you go home, Luke Silke. You never brought in the turf for your mother this morning.'

Luke knew immediately that he was back in the real world. As they walked along the narrow road home, Danielle said, 'Did all this really happen or was it some kind of dream?'

'It must have happened,' David replied, looking at the Key to Time still in his hand.

They all turned and looked back at the beach. The tunnel had disappeared and the beach was quiet and deserted. Chloe looked at the key in confusion, while the others were puzzled as to why Janus had not come to retrieve it.

Before anyone could say another word, Luke blurted out, 'We'll worry about that later!' He began to run ahead of the others and called out, 'Come on, give us a hand with the turf before my ma loses the head entirely!'

Acknowledgments

Sincere thanks to the following people for reading this book and also for their excellent advice and encouragement: Anne Maria Furey, Pamela O'Hanlon, Grace O'Hanlon, Marita Silke, Mary Henry, Robert 'Bob' Waller, Eamon Howley, Colga O'Dea, Rob Howse, Jennifer Murphy, Laura Walsh, Jenna Moylan, Dale Moylan, Emma Reems, Josephine O'Farrell, Mary O'Holleran, Bernadette Murphy, Naomi Jane Zettl, James Casserly, Fiona Graham, Danielle Furey, Patrick Fallon, Ciara Thornton, Colin Finnerty, Martin Lynch, Nicola Lynch, Max Lynch, Amy Josephine Lynch, Seán Glynn, David O'Brien, Martin Carr, Deirdre Carr, Aoife Carr, Sinéad Carr, Siobhán Carr, Jacqueline O'Brien, Evin Hynes, Anna Carroll, Rebecca Flannery, Jenny Flannery, Shane Traynor, Christian O'Connor, Brendan O'Hara, Sarah Gillespie, Galway City Museum, James Harold, Galway Arts Office, Maura Ó Crónín, Galway Early Music.

Again, thanks to my wife Noreen and children, Patrick, David and Lisa, for all their support and encouragement.

By the same Author:

*The Shimmering Waste: The Life and
Times of Robert O'Hara Burke*

The Lynch Family of Galway

Role of Honour: The Mayors of Galway City 1485–2001

Mervue 1955–2003

The Galway Arms Golfing Society

Fields of Slaughter: The Battle of Knockdoe 1504

Supreme Sacrifice: The Story of Eamonn Ceannt 1881–1916

Galway and the Great War

Forgotten Heroes: Galway Soldiers of the Great War 1914–1918

Galway's Great War Memorial Book 1914–1918

OTHER INTERESTING TITLES

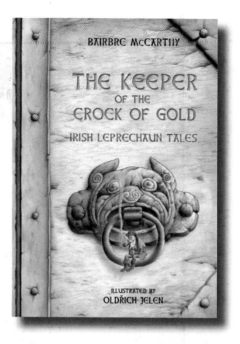

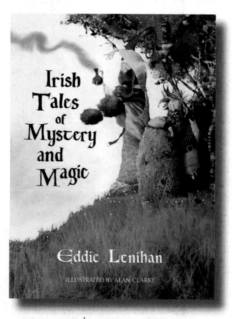